BLOOD
ON HIS
HANDS

Published by Lethe Press
lethepressbooks.com
ISBN: 978-1-59021-729-0

BLOOD ON HIS HANDS

Edited by
Michael Carte

LETHE
PRESS

Contents

Introduction

Michael Carte

Remember the first time you were bitten. The first time the guy you were infatuated with nibbled on a finger, an earlobe. Did he catch your lower lip between his teeth as the kissing grew more intense, rougher? Or maybe his mouth bruised the skin of your neck. Think back to that moment when you surrendered, that shudder crawling up and down your spine. You feared being devoured by him. And, at the same time, a part of you wanted to be eaten.

Maybe you were the aggressive lover. You realized that kissing was not nearly enough; you needed the satisfaction of taking a bit of flesh into your mouth, to discover what its taste could be if you truly bit down. Hard.

When did you discover the truth: that incisors are erogenous?

Me? I was eighteen, pledging a fraternity freshman year at Tulane. Daniel, the brother mentoring me, brought me along one hot night to serve as a lookout while he stole hood ornaments from the cars parked on the streets around campus. He planned to give every girl in his favorite sorority a bit of chrome. I watched as he grabbed ahold of an old Cadillac's hood ornament with his bare hands and began to wrench it loose. But his sweaty grip slipped, and the metallic wreath sliced open his palm.

He shucked off his shirt, and together we tore it apart. I wrapped the makeshift bandage around his palm. He did not want to go to the emergency room; he wanted to drink more beer. I understood this pressing need; I knew about thirst.

A brother drove us to the hospital in his old pickup. Three-speed manual transmission and no air-conditioning. In the back, Daniel tipped back his last bottle of Kürten, and the sweat dripped down his round face and neck, darkening the tufts of chest hair. He handed me the bottle. I tasted blood on its neck from what had soaked through his bandage. Coppery tang, salty on my tongue. Better than the bite of hops.

How could I not crave more?

After the stitches and a dose of Percocet, he stumbled up the rickety fraternity house steps to his room on the second floor. From behind, I pushed him; my fingertips slid up and down the damp curve of his bare back. Drowsy, he tried to open the mini-fridge, but I pushed him onto the mattress. The bedding looked it had yet to be changed that semester. As I pulled off his sneakers, Daniel struggled to sit upright, his wounded hand brushing across my face. A new instinct rose inside me, possessed me. I grabbed his wrist and brought his palm to my mouth, pressing the gauze to my lips. I straddled Daniel. With a knee on his chest, I kept him supine as I began tearing at the bandage with my teeth. When my tongue found the sutures, he started to moan. My lips soon became wet, ruddy. Drops fell down. I heard him moan. Assent. Surrender. I soaked my boxers. He soaked the bed.

The other brothers believed that Daniel was so wasted that he ripped open his stitches. He did not challenge this, but would never remain long in the same room as me after that. We were never alone together again. After initiation, I refused to live at the fraternity house. My new roommate was a gangly, naive mouse who fainted at the sight of blood. I believed I would be safe from temptation.

But I could never keep a promise. Not to myself, especially—while alive, I always broke Lent.

And when the fraternity gave me a little brother, a fresh pledge of my own to oversee—a Midwestern boy, like me, a wrestler with a squint and thick neck—didn't I lick my lips? And after a night drunken carousing, I brought him back to the apartment I shared with my roommate. And wasn't it kind of me to let him rinse off the Louisiana heat? Would he have agreed if he had known I would break the latch on the bathroom door? Or that, I would pull off the shower curtain from its cheap plastic hooks?

He must have thought he was being hazed as I grabbed one arm. A lump of pale-green soap fell to the tub floor. Then my other hand pressed against his stomach, my fingers daring to touch his thick pubes. By his third week, a pledge is conditioned to never say "No," to a brother. His shoulder tasted of Irish Spring. Until I broke the skin.

My fretful roommate Steve soon came home to find the pledge sitting sullenly on the sofa and tugging at the hem and collar and cuffs of an old dress shirt of mine, desperate to hide the bite marks. At the time, Steve thought I merely fucked the pledge—as did the brothers, who expelled me.

Since those raucous and raunchy college days, my old roommate has repeatedly begged me ... to make amends, I think, for the many monstrous things I did while we lived together in New Orleans. Reluctantly, I collected these thirteen tales at his behest.

And that is why you happen to be holding a book about men and monsters … I can vouch that often they are one and the same.

New Orleans is truly the American Transylvania. Always plenty to drink there. And vampires are always thirsty, yet never satisfied. Their nights they spend prowling, much like the boys or men who set foot out of doors to find stolen moments of pleasure, like my fraternity brothers. While they bit off more than they could chew, I did not.

There are pleasures, bloody and dark, to be found in these stories, and they are often rich to the taste. Take the word of a dead man.

Bloodletting

Greg Herren

The damp air was thick with the scent of blood.

It had been days since I had last fed, and the desire was gnawing at my insides. I stood up, and my eyes focused on a young man walking a bicycle in front of the cathedral. He was talking on a cell phone, his face animated and agitated. He was wearing a T-shirt that read *Who Dat Say They Gonna Beat Dem Saints?* and a pair of ratty old paint-spattered jeans cut off at the knees. There was a tattoo of Tweety on his right calf and another indistinguishable one on his left forearm. His hair was dark, combed to a peak in the center of his head, and his face was flushed. He stopped walking, his voice getting louder and louder as his face got darker.

I could smell his blood. I could almost hear his beating heart.

I could see the pulsing vein in his neck beckoning me forward.

The sun was setting, and the lights around Jackson Square were starting to come on. The tarot card readers were folding their tables, ready to disappear into the night. The band playing in front of the cathedral was putting their instruments away. The artists who hung their work on the iron fence around the park were long gone, as were the living statues. The square, so teeming with life just a short hour earlier, was emptying of people, and the setting sun was taking the warmth with it as it slowly disappeared in the west. The cold breeze from the river ruffled my hair as I watched the young man with the bicycle. He started wheeling the bicycle forward, still talking on the phone. He reached the concrete ramp leading up to Chartres Street. He stopped just as he reached the street, and I focused my hearing as he became more agitated. *What do you want me to say? You're just being a bitch, and anything I say, you're just going to turn around on me.*

I felt the burning inside.

Desire was turning into need.

I knew it was best to satisfy the desire before it became a need. I could feel the knots of pain from deprivation forming behind each of my temples and knew it was almost too late. I shouldn't have let it go this long, but I wanted to test my limits and see how long I could put off the hunger. I'd been taught to feed daily, which would keep the hunger under control and keep me out of danger.

Need was dangerous. Need led a vampire to take risks he wouldn't take ordinarily. And risks could lead to exposure, to a painful death.

The first lesson I'd learned was to always satiate the hunger while it was still desire, and never let it become need.

I had waited too long.

He started walking again, and I began following him, focusing on the curve of his buttocks in his jeans. The T-shirt was a little too small, riding up on his back so I could see the dimples in his lower back just above the swell of his ass. He was a little more slender than I liked, but it didn't matter since I wasn't going to fuck him. I was just going to pierce his neck for a moment and drink from his veins until the desire faded, and I returned to my normal state.

You haven't been normal in over two years, a voice inside my head whispered.

I ignored it.

He crossed St. Ann Street and continued up Chartres, still talking on the phone, completely oblivious to everything and everyone around him. There weren't many people on Chartres Street as darkness continued falling on the Quarter. I felt power surging through my body with each step I took. The darkness is the vampire's friend, making us even more powerful, stronger. My eyes adjusted to the darkness. At first, the clarity of my night vision always caught me off guard, but now I was used to it. I started walking faster, figuring I could catch up to him and pull him into one of the many shadowed doorways. Anyone passing by would assume we were simply enjoying a public display of affection—and the groans of pleasure he would emit as I drained off some of his blood would give further proof to the lie.

The blood scent was so strong I could almost taste it, the need rising in me, and I knew I had to catch him soon—

"Cord?"

I froze, stopped walking.

"My God, it *is* you." A hand grabbed my arm from behind and spun me around. "I—I thought you were *dead,* man."

"Let me go," I growled, the need beginning to push everything else out of my mind, and I was dangerously close to losing control.

"No way, man!" My old roommate from Beta Kappa, Jared Holcomb, was smiling at me. His entire face lit up with a smile the way it always had. His thick blond hair was longer than I remembered, and his muscles were thicker, stronger. He wore a tight pair of low-rise jeans and a blue shirt that hugged his torso. "Where have you been? My God... I'm so glad to see you!"

Always feed before the desire becomes a need, my maker, Jean-Paul, had lectured me over and over again. *When it becomes a need, you cannot control yourself, and you will take risks you usually don't; you put yourself at risk.*

It was too late.

I grabbed Jared with both hands and pulled him into an unlit doorway, wrapping my arms around him and pressing my body against his. He made a shocked noise, squirming a bit before I sank my teeth into his neck and drank.

I could feel my cock hardening. I could feel Jared's dick start to stiffen against mine as he began to moan as the delicious warm blood filled my mouth from the little wounds I'd made, as his precious life force entered my body.

I pulled my head back, wiping at my mouth, gasping.

Jared remained leaning against the door, his breath coming in shallow gulps. His eyes were half-closed, and blood was dribbling down his neck from the holes I'd left in his throat. I took a few steps back and checked the street. There was no one nearby or closer than Jackson Square a half-block away.

"Fuck," I muttered under my breath. I'd gotten lucky. I shook my head, furious at myself. What if he hadn't been alone? What if someone had come walking along at just the right moment, or a police car had come around the corner at St. Ann just as I grabbed him?

When desire becomes need, a vampire forgets everything but the blood. He makes mistakes, takes risks he shouldn't— and frequently gets caught. It must never become need, else you risk everything. Most vampires are caught—and killed—when they've gone too long without feeding. Don't let that happen to you.

I must have been crazy to let it go so long—especially when there were always people about in the Quarter to feed on. What had I been thinking?

You weren't thinking, that's the problem, I scolded myself. *Seeing how long you could go? That's madness and a one-way ticket to death.*

I shook my head again, pricked my right index finger with one of my teeth, and rubbed my blood over the two little holes the way Jean-Paul had shown me.

The holes didn't close the way they usually did. I stared at the wounds. It couldn't be. They *always* healed.

I could feel the panic rising in me as I rubbed more of my blood over the punctures. I heard myself muttering, "Come on, come on, come on," over and over again, but the wounds weren't healing the way they were supposed to. Instead, Jared's blood continued to seep out through them, dribbling down his neck and staining his shirt. The pale blue was turning dark just below the collar, where the running blood came into contact with the tightly fitting cotton. His nipples were erect, and all of his weight was leaning back against the wall. His eyes opened a little wider yet were still half-closed. Other than the bleeding neck, he looked like so many others who drank more than they should in the Quarter. They weren't focused and looked a little cloudy to me.

"What—?" He swallowed, his throat working, the Adam's apple bobbing up and down. "Wha—happen? Cord? I feel—I feel funny."

I couldn't just leave him there, with his neck bleeding and his shirt getting darker with wetness every passing second. Something was wrong, something was seriously wrong, and

I had to get away as quickly as possible, but I couldn't just leave him there.

Modern society might not believe in vampires, but when the police found him—and he would certainly wind up in the hands of the police—they might not go for the notion of a vampire attack, but I couldn't take the risk he would remember seeing me, and mention me to the cops.

And since Cord Logan had died in a fire two years earlier on Lundi Gras, that was a can of worms best left unopened.

I put his left arm around my shoulders and placed his head on my neck. At least the wounds were hidden that way, and in the growing darkness, no one would notice the bloody shirt. "Come on, buddy, you need to walk with me," I whispered to him.

His head tilted back for a moment, and his face lit up with a crazy grin. "Buddy, I knew you weren't dead. I told them all you weren't dead."

"Come on, it's just a couple of blocks." I smiled into his eyes, willing him to start walking. "Use me for support if you can't stand up."

"Okay," he replied, and started walking. Most of his weight was on me, and had I been a mortal, we probably would have both fallen to the ground. But I was no longer mortal, and while I had not matured into my full strength as a vampire—Jean-Paul said it would take another fifty or so mortal years for that to happen—I was still stronger than I'd been a twenty-year-old college student. We shuffled our way past the Presbytere, but no one really paid attention to us. It was a common sight in the Quarter—Jared looked like another young man who'd had too much to drink and needed to be helped back to his hotel. We turned and headed down the alley between the Presbytere and the Cathedral. The alley was empty and silent other than our footsteps against the stone. Even though I was stronger, I was still having trouble drawing breath by the time we reached Royal Street. We headed up to Orleans, passed the crowds on Bourbon, and the dancing hand grenade in front of Tropical Isle. Before I knew it, I was helping up the steps of Jean-Paul's house. I put the key in the lock and helped him inside, setting him down on the couch.

I stared at the little cottage across the street as I turned to shut and lock the front door.. It was still in the process of being rebuilt after the fire. It was there tht Jean-Paul had rescued me from the witch Sebastian and brought my dying body back across the street to his house. It was on that very couch where Jared now lay that Jean-Paul had opened the vein in his arm and had me drink his blood, the blood that transformed me into what I am now, no longer human. I shut the door and drew the curtains shut, flipping the light switch. The overhead chandelier came to life, casting strange shadows into every corner.

I knelt down beside Jared. His eyes were now fully closed, and his breathing became shallow. His skin felt cold, and I pressed my fingers against his wrist. His heart was beating, but not strongly. The wounds on his neck had stopped bleeding but still were open and angry. I put my hand up to my mouth in order to open another wound in a finger but stopped.

Think about it, Cord, you must be doing something wrong. You've done this a thousand times, and it always, always works.

But as much as I thought about it, hard as I tried to remember, there was nothing else I could remember doing differently I wasn't doing now. It was simple—you merely opened a wound and rubbed some of your own blood over the mortal's wounds. Within seconds, those wounds would close just as your own would. I shook my head and punctured my thumb.

I pressed my thumb over his wounds, rubbed gently, and pulled my thumb away. Even as the wound in my own thumb closed, the wounds in Jared's neck remained clearly visible.

I took a deep breath and tried not to panic.

Jared opened his eyes again and smiled weakly. "I knew you weren't dead." He reached up with a cool hand and touched the side of my face. "I just knew. Everyone said you were dead, they had a funeral and everything, but I knew." His face clouded with confusion. "But how…I don't understand…"

"Shhhh," I whispered, my mind racing as I tried to figure out what to do.

This was precisely why Jean-Paul had forbidden me to return to New Orleans. He was right again, as usual. *Yes, I know you're not from there, but you know people who are, and they all think you're dead. You cannot risk going back there. What are you going to do if one of them sees you? How are you going to explain being alive? There is no explanation, Cord, and you will have to kill them.*

And even though Jared had been one of my best friends, one of my fraternity brothers, I knew if Jean-Paul knew what was happening, he would order me to kill Jared. Kill him and make sure the body was never found.

If you don't kill him, you risk exposing yourself. And everyone else in the vampire world—is that what you want, Cord? To prove to them vampires DO exist? They would hunt us all down and kill us. It's either him or us, Cord. You know what you have to do.

"I feel funny," Jared said, shifting around on the couch and his eyes opened even further. They weren't as glassy and focus-less as earlier; that was a step in the right direction.

Maybe he would recover normally.

I placed my fingers back on his wrist. His pulse felt stronger.

The wounds on his neck were scabbing over.

That was a step in the right direction, but it's still not normal. My blood should have healed the damned things! What was wrong? Maybe Jared somehow was different than other humans?

But that didn't make any sense.

"Kiss me," Jared whispered, smiling at me.

"What?" I stared at him. "You can't be serious."

"I want you," he whispered. His lips spread in a smile. "I've always wanted you, Cord. Always."

I gulped. In the three years at Ole Miss I'd known Jared, I'd never once gotten the slightest inkling he was gay, or even the least bit curious. We'd pledged together, shared a room at the house, and been as close as brothers. Jared was the only person in the house I'd come out to—and he'd been supportive, even going with me to Memphis to a gay bar. It had been Jared's idea to come to stay with his parents for Mardi Gras and it helped me break away from the other fraternity brothers who'd also come down so I could go to the gay bars. Neither of us had any way of knowing the trip would result in my becoming a vampire—well, Jared just thought I'd been killed, burned to death in the fire. I'd always been attracted to Jared but never considered acting on it—no matter how drunk or high either of us might have been.

And it was very tempting.

"Jared—"

He licked his lips. "I was too much of a coward to ever do anything. That time we went to the bar in Memphis... I wanted to kiss you that night. It broke my heart when you died, Cord. And now you're alive. I'm not going to miss this chance. I've been sorry ever since you died. I never had the courage to do anything with you." He smiled again. "But now you aren't dead." He reached out and touched my hair. "Somehow, I knew you weren't. I knew that wasn't you in that house."

Tears filled my eyes. Oh, how I'd longed to hear those words from him! How I'd longed to kiss him, to put my arms around him, to put my mouth on his cock, to let him fill me up with his. But this didn't feel right somehow, it was wrong, like somehow my biting him and sucking his blood had done this to him—was making him think and react in a way that wasn't natural to him.

But his wounds hadn't healed, either. That wasn't natural, either.

He reached up and kissed me. It felt like an electrical current ran through my body. Not even kissing Jean-Paul had felt like this.

I was aware of my cock growing hard inside my jeans, and as Jared's tongue slipped in between my lips and inside my mouth, I could see in my head that he was getting hard too. I reached down and caressed the thick hardness beneath the denim, and he moaned, never removing his tongue from inside my mouth. He began stroking my chest with his hands, pulling and tweaking at my erect and sensitive nipples, and I pushed him back down on the couch, climbing on top of him, our hips beginning to move back and forth as we ground our crotches into each other.

I pulled my mouth away from his lips. He smiled up at me. "I love you, Cord," he breathed, "I always have."

Jean-Paul never said that to me. I wanted to believe him.

Still, in spite of how badly I wanted him, the animalistic need driving me, I couldn't shake the sense that something, somehow, was not right about this.

His hands came up, caressing my hardness through my pants, and my desire pushed all other thoughts out of my mind.

I reached down and undid my pants, freeing my cock. Jared smiled at me and licked his thumb. He started running it over the head of my cock.

"Ooooooh," I moaned.

I pushed my pants down, as he kept rubbing away. Unable to stand it anymore, I grabbed the front of his pants and pulled, the riveted buttons holding his fly closed, popping and flying away. I got to my knees and yanked his pants down, freeing his long beautiful cock. As I yanked, I heard the denim tearing, and once they were free, I tossed them aside like torn rags. I reached for the bottle of lube and squirted it onto his erection.

"I want to be inside you," he breathed as I mounted him, spreading my butt cheeks and lowering myself on top of his cock.

The pressure against my anus was sharp and painful, then my muscles relaxed, and I slid down, feeling his urgency filling me. I gasped and moaned as I continued to slide, settling down onto him when I felt his thick balls pressing against my cheeks.

His entire body began to tremble, his eyes closing partway as I started moving up and down. He tried to push up into me as I went upwards, but I held his hips down with my hands. He struggled against my strength at first, to no avail. I was much stronger than he—he had no idea how strong, nor did I want him to find out. I was still not completely used to how much power my muscles now contained, and I was afraid I might accidentally hurt him.

"Your ass is amazing," he whispered, tugging on my nipples and sending electricity through my body. "It feels so good; please don't stop."

I smiled. The pleasure was so intense I couldn't stop had I wanted to. I reached down and stroked his chest, and his entire body convulsed, bucking upwards. The thrusts were strong, intense, and it felt as though I was being split in two.

I cried out, my head going back as he continued driving up into me. My entire mind was being consumed with the pleasure from his cock, which felt as though it were burning inside of me. No one had ever fucked me this way, not Jean-Paul, not any of the others in our little fraternity of vampires. The passion, the power—my eyes began to lose focus, and everything in front of me seemed seared with white. I was vaguely aware that he was forcing my backwards, never stopping with the thrusting, not once relenting. The pleasure, my God, the pleasure, and I was on my back. He was on top of me, and in the mirror behind him I could see his powerful back, the fleur-de-lis tattoo on his right shoulder blade, his beautiful round white ass clenching and unclenching as he drove into me, as though he were trying to get his cock so deep inside me it might never come out, and I wanted him inside me, I wanted to feel his entire body consumed inside of mine, and the thrusting and driving to never stop....

And his lips were at my own throat, moving from the base of my chin to the hollow where my neck met my chest, his tongue darting out and dancing against my skin.

And it went on, the pleasure building inside of me until I could barely stand it any longer—

And his head went back, and he screamed as his body went rigid, and I could feel him squirting inside of me, his body convulsing and racking with the pleasure with each spurt—

And my own splashed out of me, raining onto my chest and my face and into my hair.

He convulsed a few more times, then collapsed on top of me, his energy spent.

I lay there panting for a moment or two, enjoying his weight and warmth on top of me.

His breathing shallowed and became even, and I gently pushed him aside, feeling his softening penis slide out of me. I slid out and gently rolled him over onto his back, staring at his beauty as he lay there in the soft glow of moonlight coming through the stained glass just above the house's front door.

Blood still oozed from the wounds on his neck.

I grabbed a towel and wiped myself off, then spit onto my fingers. I rubbed them over the wounds, but the wounds did not close.

I don't understand —it has always worked; what is wrong. What is so different about this time that the wounds will not close?

He started murmuring in his sleep, tossing a bit on the couch.

I walked over to the front windows and opened the red velvet curtains a bit, looking at the house across the street— the house where I'd almost died, a victim of the desires of the mixed-race witch, Sebastian, and his thirst to combine the power of the vampire with his own witchcraft. I closed my eyes and remembered being tied to the bed while Sebastian violated my body and went through the mysterious ritual I had not understood until Jean-Paul and the others had come to my rescue. I remembered the feeling of dying, of my body going cold as Jean-Paul wrapped me in a blanket and carried me out of the house and back across the street, and the metallic taste of his blood as he fed me in order to save me.

I tried to remember if my own wounds from him had closed that first night he had fed on me, that night when I'd run into him and his friends at Oz while the madness of Carnival raged in the streets of the French Quarter.

Perhaps I'd taken too much from him. Maybe that was why the wounds wouldn't heal. Jean-Paul and the others always warned me about taking too much—but they never said why.

I started to turn away from the window when something flickered in one of the windows across the street. I spun my head back, but whatever it was, was no longer there.

Now you're imagining things. There's no one there; the house isn't habitable yet.

Jared moaned in his sleep, and I walked back over to the couch. I knelt beside him, marveling again at how beautiful he was. I'd always had a crush on him back at the fraternity house, but he was straight—he'd made that very clear to me.

Then why did he—it doesn't make any sense. Was it the connection forged when I took his blood? His life force? There's so much you still don't know about all of this, Jean-Paul was right, you should have stayed in Palm Springs with him and the others.

"I don't feel so good," he barely whispered as I started stroking his forehead again. "What—what have you done to me, Cord?" He shifted again on the couch. "So cold, so very, very cold."

I allowed my other hand to come up and press on the jugular vein in his throat. The heartbeat was weak and faint.

I've killed him.

I felt tears rising in my eyes.

I raised my wrist to my mouth and bit into the artery there. As my own blood began to flow over my skin, I lowered my wrist to his mouth.

I heard Jean-Paul's voice in my head. *You are too young to this life to create another, such as ourselves. Your heart isn't strong enough yet, so you must never ever try to turn a human until such time as I tell you that you can.*

But he would die unless....

"Drink," I whispered, parting his lips and allowing my blood to run onto his tongue.

Jared's eyes opened at the first taste of my blood, and color began to return to his cheeks. He closed his mouth around the holes in my wrist and began to suckle.

I closed my eyes and allowed my head to fall backward.

Jean-Paul's voice became almost mocking. *You cannot control yourself, and you will take risks you usually don't; you put yourself at risk.*

Whatever the risks, I had to take them.

Outlaws & Bad Men

Kenzie Mathews

I was hitchin' on the wrong side of the Mississippi when
he picked me up in a black 1970 Chevy Impala that'd seen
much better days. I looked up and down the road. The Impala
was the first I'd seen in hours since leaving the country gas
mart. Chances were slim to none that I'd get a better ride.
He reached over to open the door, and I glanced in. He was
a clean-cut, J-Crew model pretty: sandy blonde hair cut
short, small square-rimmed glasses, strong classic nose
and chin. He wasn't me typical hustle, but I thought wtf?
Beggers canna be choosers.

Something nineties rock and growly played on the
radio, and that decided me. I got in. Got a real hard-on for
American grunge and metal. Brings 'round good memories,
and I've been finding good times most rare and fine. The
impala roared down the empty country highway. Neither of
us had said where we were going, but I guess it didn't really
matter in the long run anyway. We didn't know where we
were going. We didn't have any place to be.

I figured I could at least get a meal out of him, maybe a decent fuck and a shower. God knew I needed a shower. I pulled the visor down to check the mirror. You'd think it'd come to naught, but some of those tales are just made up. Mirror showed me: a man with dark eyes rimmed red, shoulder-length, greasy black hair, angled bone face, pale skin, and a girl's mouth looked back at me.

Ah, yes, the road could get nasty, the nights tacky and long, but those incubus looks would follow me. Always a good fuck, me. And if you miss something necessary the next day, say your wallet or your wedding ring or maybe a pint or two, well, there was always the memory of my girlish mouth and long thick cock to persuade you to leave the cops out of it.

"Chase," me driver said.

I grinned at him, "Lochlan."

Chase glanced at me, startled. "Irish?"

"Yea."

"Are you here on a work visa?"

I chuckled. "Somet'ing like that."

Chase was silent only a moment, one hand's fingers tapping the wheel. "Did it expire?"

I looked out the window, closing my eyes for a short lay-down. "Dunno. You a cop or somet'ing?"

Now, it was his turn to chuckle, like a small rumble in his chest just as sleep was taking me. "Yeah," he said, "Something like that."

I must've fell asleep because it was the same dream I've been waking up screaming to for near ten years now: blood on me hands, in me mouth, on me body, and worse, that spill, that gush that painted the walls and floor. I slip in it, wet black gore clinging to me naked body, sliding down me chest, back, and legs. I drunk-stumble walk, crying out for Ma. For this is not me flat in Dublin, no. This is my old room in me old home, in me old small town and me folks, me little sister, are here somew'ere.

I find them after I reach the end of the hall. Like a sick fuckin' joke, they are, their t'roats ripped out, their guts spilling onto their laps. They sit there, holdin' hands liked they're watching the tellie. Rigor mortis has set in, keepin' the bodies propped. Flies circle, buzzing. I fall to me knees and cry like a baby, staring at them til I remember me little sister.

I tear the house apart lookin' for her. Search the backyard. Call around on the phone. Check her room. She's left her school backpack on her bed. Day crumbles into evenin' and, I go to the icebox for one of Da's beers.

She's there, me little sister. Cut into parts like Chinese take-out.

I fall again to the floor, screamin', losin' me mind entirely, unable to turn away from her dead staring eyes. And then, at last, when I'm done with the human part that's left... I give into the hunger and become the monster everyone always said I'd be.

That's when I knew: the monster will always win and there wasna not'ing I could do to stop it. To stop me.

It's a most terrible dream, and worse, it's true. It makes me sick and want to kill meself but then, the monster in me, he likes livin' don't he? Cos it's a full ten year later and I'm still walkin the earth, carryin' me bad dreams and doin' bad t'ings.

I somet'imes remember me little sister's face. But not often. Not often.

*

I woke now with his hand rubbing me cock. Me jeans clung to me wetly, and me cock was risin', most appreciative of his attentions. He grinned at me, J-Crew American, somet'ing like a cop, what's his fuckin' name again? Ah, yea, Chase. We're in some parkin' lot, parked right up next to some great public buildin'. I widened me legs a little to give him full range to me cock. I put me hand on his to guide him a little. I love the risk of bein' found out. I like an audience.

"Not just yet," He said slowly, removing his hand. He jerked his head sideways, motionin' towards the large stone buildin'. "I need you to keep the car running. Can you drive?"

"Yea, but what's your rush?"

Chase grinned wider. "My rush is coming." And he got out of the car, carrying a large duffle bag like somet'ing you take to the gym. Gave me a shiny slick grin and pulled out a fleshy mask from his jean's back pocket. He pulled it over his head and shot me a peace symbol. Now, he's the Wolf-Man. Beauty. I gave him a double thump up him with a mockin' snarl. WTF? Whatever. His rush.

I slid over to the driver's seat and watched him go up the long stairs and into the buildin'. I was sittin' there for the longest time and startin' to get mighty bored when he came runnin' back out with the gym bag, now fat and heavy. He was practically screaming with laughter.

Two security came swinging out the front doors and started shooin' at the car, at Chase. At me. Chase slid over the car hood, landing hard on the ot'er side, and he's barely in when the front shield bursts under gunshot. I gunned the car, and we shoot forward as the guards run down the stairs and into the street to shoot at us.

We're a good five blocks away, when I heard the first sirens. Chase thrusted his forearm in my face, pointing somew'ere out the window. In this time, he's taken off his mask, and now he's back to being just Joe Criminal again. "Park there!"

I pulled into the Motel 6 parking lot, and before the car even stopped, Chase was out and lookin' for another ride. By the time I reached him, he'd jimmied the lock on a sporty Jeep. He jumped in and hot-wired the car, jerking wires outta the dash underside. I stepped to the other side, waiting til the car roared into life. It was a bit of a wait then before he unlocked me side of the car, kinda like he wanna too sure he wanted me to come along for the ride.

Felt a little vulnerable. I'm so used to being the hustler, it was odd to be on the other side of it. He stared at me, and I dunno if it was me fine looks or the meetin' of monsters, but he reached over and let me in. I shut the door just in time, for he sped off then in the opposite direction. We passed several cop cars going the wrong way. But, we were free now, out in the world and up to no good.

We burned our way out of town and ran further, down the highway til the adredeline would let us breathe evenly and then, he found the first turnoff he came across. He couldn't get my ragin' cock in his mouth fast enough and he sucked me dry, bringin' me to a whimper, a hollowin' that felt like I was dry desert inside, scraped clean, my balls empty and tight. I returned the favor, nearly devourin' his head, me saliva numbin' his cock to my needle teeth, me tongue strokin' and cradlin'. I sucked him til he jerked, and then I licked him clean. Sometimes the blood bothers them, gets them worried.

You'd not see them if you wanted to—me needle teeth, they hide behind me canines. I call them needles for the obvious: they withdraw and take and I need it to live. It's best though if the blood is mixed with cum. Has to do with the salt and the cream of it all. It's like a meal and dessert all at once.

He's weak now, Chase. I nodded my head towards the back. Take a lie down. I'll drive.

He smiled at me. Reached out and cradled my jaw and ear. It was almost painful, his grip hard and cruel. I can see his monster playin' in his eyes. "I meant to leave you there. Give me more time to get away."

I whispered, "But you didna," and lean into the pain. Me needle teeth throb. We like a little hurt now and again. To give, to take. It blurs the lines in me head.

"No, I didna," Chase returned, mockin' my accent. He climbed over the seat and took himself a lie down. His voice muffled, his arm pointing in a random direction, he said, "Drive that way."

I pressed and wrapped the loose wires, starting the Jeep. I drove that way.

After a long time, I pulled over and listened to Chase snore. I reached back and pushed on him a bit. He didna wake. He snored on. Figurin' now was better than later or never, I leaned over the seat and searched him. He slept on, as sweet and trustin' as a wee lamb. I found his wallet in the inside pocket of his jacket. I left one credit card, but I took the others as they were not as obvious, packed behind the first. I also found a few driver's licenses. Chase was beginning to stir, so I left the first license there and took the others. My my my, Chase was a most interestin' fella. Chase was back to snorin' by the time I got back onto the highway.

There was an older man once who took me in. He lived in a palace. Most Americans do, though. I'm used to smaller, tighter places. Older. Here, though, Americans are so young, brash, and the places they try to fill are huge, which seems to make them smaller if you are askin' me. He picked me up in a pub. I'd gone for a drink and a pint or two. Water closets are my forte. What man doesn't want his cocked sucked in the privacy of the privy? Hard to find... I crack meself up. But, it's true. Many a straight man has gone crooked in lavatory. Found himself bent. Is there anyt'ing sweeter than innocence, ignorance corrupted in a foul place? I dunno why it appeals so.

But, I was there, on my knees in piss givin' a time to some tattooed punk and taking me drink and pint or two while he weaved and danced his hips in me mouth, filling me mouth with his seed, and me soul with his life's blood. A good exchange, in'it? A moment's deep pleasure that keeps me alive and suckin'. Til the day I die.

I'm not too sure I'll die. I think that part of the tales is true. And I'm not courtin' it, no, but still. I look the same I did the day I murdered and ate me family. Not a stone gained 'round me waist, not a gray hair in me head. It may be I'll be young and beautiful forever. Fate's cruel to most but been kind to me monster.

And the old tosser came in and watched. I like an audience. I play up to it. I had the punk cryin' and cradlin' me head, beggin' for me number, for me to come home with him and I stood up instead, laughin', his come and blood coating me glistenin' lips. The old man gave me a hundred-dollar bill to wipe me mouth with. And with him, I went.

It was a white, clean, beautiful American palace. Swept out, scrubbed, and toiled over daily by slave women he'd bought on the underground black market. This was the first glimpse I had of his monster. I saw more of his monster in the times following. He didna bring others over much unless they knew they'd keep his secrets. Obviously, he knew he could buy me silence. He never slept with his slave women, but he let others buy them for a time or more. This was one of the many reasons I hated him.

Other than me family, I've worked hard to keep me victims alive. It's a cage for me monster, I know, for he'd like not'in' better than carnage and bloodshed. And maybe it started out selfish: ten years of that nightmare night over and over again while I sleep. I canna take more of that. I know I may not always win and one day, me monster will overcome me but…but still I try. I'm the one who has to look at that good lookin' fella in the mirror.

But this man's victims were dead-alive. It was unspeakable cruelty. And he was enjoyin' himself immensely. I planned to call the cops on him once I was out. Put a stop to him, I would. But, I needed a nicer wallet to get about. This was me truest downfall: me practical side, me daily life livin' side. We canna all get about livin' on blood and sex alone, you know.

At the start of it, he wined and dined me. It was familiar and ho-hum. I ate his fine bland foods, I drank his tasteful yet tasteless wine. I sucked him in the slow gentle worshipful way he liked, and he fucked me in the hard brisk way he liked. I took a little blood here and there to keep alive, to keep him unawares, to pad my wallet a bit for my eventual walkin' out. And then, one fine bright morn—and that's another part of the tales that falls untrue, for we can walk in daylight like saints without a-burning. One fine bright morn, I set off to walk out with my fat wallet and fat well-fed body, ready for new adventure and darker younger blood.

The old man hit me with his golf club at the front door.

Then, he and Jeeves or whatever the fuck, his fuckin' butler dragged me down to the basement dungeon where they broke in the slave women. I woke up with a chained dog collar around me bloody neck, strapped in a fuckin' torture chair.

And this is how I know that no matter what, me sweet looks will return the next day. And I maybe will live forever.

I will not speak of the t'ings they did to me, of the instruments they used on me, of the fuckin'and suckin' that I did or was done onto. I took a bite here and again, the times I could, the bits I could. Not that I wanted to live and endure more, but I was starvin' and hunger's never met shame. I lived on, and they grew tired and filled with wonder at me. They stopped feedin me entirely, and the hunger built up until the monster raged within me. And then, Jeeves or what the fuck, he thought me weak, for I was, but the monster was hidin' and peerin' out, waitin' his chances. Jeeves unwrapped me from the table I now lived on, rolled me to the ground, and started another rapin'.

Me monster woke up and filled me stomachs.

The old man, ever the audience, he, watched it happen and coolly dropped a silver plug into my thigh. That is somet'ing the old tales speak of for another monster, but it worked on mine all the same. I howled, clutching me thigh, rolling out from under Jeeves or what the fuck. The old man dragged me arms up and chained them to the table with tiny silver chains. Bloody chains, if not for the silver, I'd a-broken them in seconds. He let me have me lie down there, on the cold stone floor. And then, for his amusement, he kept me broken with pain and hungry or he fed me... his slaves.

There have been black times in me life. This was one of the blackest.

He knew what I was. He was tryin' to keep his women enslaved for eternity, in their dead-alive state, in his special hell. And I was helpin' him, unable to stop, unwillin' to starve. I knew soon enough, he'd ask for his own eternity, and by that time, I'd be so corrupted and sick, out of weakness I'd give it to him. So far gone a monster, me humanity a distant memory and too far out of me reach.

Worse, it would have gone on and on and on and on if a slave woman hadn't found a way out. She told the aut'orities. They came and freed the women, and then, they found me: bloody stinking, me monster exposed and horrifying, and they took pity and saw only a human man, not the monster both born and created til made worse.

They set even me free. Put me in hospital and would have taken me to court, maybe given me a new life with dignity, with meaning and purpose.

I escaped as soon as possible. The idea of exposin' everyt'ing, of being seen for what I am, was, and would always be. I just couldna. Even now, not sure if it was the exposin' of me, the monster who ate me family and drank countless others or me, the victim/accomplice who aided another monster despite meself. Donna matter. All's the same really. Shameful. Sick. Depraved. Monsters we all are.

I ran. Far away and then some.

I read in the paper that the old man was sent to life in prison. He died within a month during a riot. I hope to Jesus he's sufferin' in Hellfire now. Saints be blessed.

Come nightfall, Chase woke up hungry and asked me to find us a place. I pulled into a pancake house off the highway. Like all junkies, I need sweets. I ate chocolate chip pancakes with blueberry syrup while he had a Western Omelet with biscuits and gravy. Some of it got on his chin and before I could stop meself, I wiped it off with my thumb and put it into my mouth. Instead of panicking cos we were deep in South Fried Hilly Billy Country, Chase grinned at me. Of course he didna care, his monster loved the risky business.

I wanted to fuck him on the table right then and there. He saw it in me and we left there, big tip and all, and took to a cheap motel on the other side of the restaurant.

I fucked him deep and long, his face smashed into the bed, his fine ass in the air, my hands on his rockin' buckin' hips. He moaned into the bed, a deep bellow that raised the hairs on me body. I fucked him faster, givin' into his voice like it was a siren song. When I was spent, Chase rose up a little and took me down sideways, a quick wrestle and I gave into him, settling meself under his sweaty firm weight. His cock pressed against mine, his thigh opening me legs up a bit to keep me close. His forearms captured me head and he looked down into my eyes wonderingly.

Slowly, so slowly he kissed me, his tongue and lips exploring me mouth. I opened me mouth and gave him free reign. He took me like a hawk on prey, slow but deliberate, strong, confident. I kissed him back, echoing move for move. Chase captured me hands then, pinnin' me wrists. I arched into him, me cock still wet from plunder but willin'. His cock probed me balls, the friction excitin' me until I was beggin' by the names of the saints.

Chase reached for somet'ing on the bedside table. He whispered, "Do you trust me?"

I answered trut'fully: "No."

Chase laughed. Then, in a flash, he brought me pinned hands up over me head and he handcuffed me to the bed head. He covered me mouth as I screamed, frozen. I was stricken suddenly, thinkin' of that old man and his butler. Chase reached down with his other hand and lifted one of me legs and gently placed it over his shoulder. I was frozen still. I was thinkin' now that these kinds of thin's had to stop happenin' to me, me bein' a monster and all. And Chase got me other leg up and over his other shoulder. Then, slowly, gently if you will, he started fuckin' me. He dug in deeply and then pulled out, over and over again til the wantin' in me overcame the fear and I t'rust back into him, meetin him all the way and back again. This time, when he came, he hollered, and fell onto me, resting on my sweat damp chest.

I waited a bit for his breath to catch up and then I rattled the handcuffs.

Chase's head rose and he sat there, on me chest, starin' into me eyes. He said softly, "You'll just slow me down."

"Have I yet?"

He smiled, "Not yet but it's a matter of time. And these things go bad."

Chase sat up. He started lookin' for his clothes. I pulled on the handcuffs. They weren't too tight but they werena givin in, either. I was not in a good place. "What goes bad?"

Chase shrugged into his shirt. "We go wrong. We get caught, one of us turns on the other for a lighter sentence. I've seen it before." Chase found his jeans and pulled them on.

I rattled the handcuffs. Would they stop me monster later when hunger woke him?

"So, stop being a bad man," I said lightly as if I were bored already.

Chase stared at me for the longest time and then he looked at my cock. He smiled. Sittin' down on the bed, he reached over and started playin' with my cock. The little bastard betrayed me. I gasped, feeling pleasure and suffocation as one. Chase leaned into and whispered into my open mouth, "I can't stop being a bad man. And I can't take you with me. I'm F.B.I.I have a real life and I have to pretend to belong to it."

I jerked up, straining against the handcuffs. Chase wiped his hand on my thighs. I trembled now, my monster stirring, peering within me, lookin' for a weakness. F.B.I.?

Was he playin' me? What did he know then? Chase was an enemy and I was caught. I'd not left behind too many bodies since me family but still, there was enough to hang me, yea. And I was still wanted in Ireland. They dunno forget family massacre and cannibalism there, you know. Add to all this, if I were being watched, it'd soon be obvious that I didna age. Or was he lyin', monsters do you know.

Chase took the handcuff key out of his pocket and laid it across the bedside table. He tapped it with his finger. "I wish it was different, Lochlan from Ireland." Chase walked to the door and opened it. He turned back around there and faced me, "I wish I could fuck you for all of eternity." He smiled, shaking his head. Then, he was gone.

And the monster within me woke up even though the hunger for blood was not yet stirrin'. There was another hunger he was answerin' to.

Under the monster's careful distant observance, I broke the bones on my left hand and reached over to the bedside table for the key. Just metal, the handcuffs. Gingerly, painfully, I opened the lock on the handcuff and sat up in the bed, my right hand cradling my broken left. It hurt like hellfire but I knew with the monster's guidance that I'd soon knit it up tight in bandages and go on like nothin' was wrong. That was the monster within, always persistent, waitin'silently for the right time to pounce.

The monster then said out-loud, "Well, then, I'm guessin' you'll be getting your wishes filled, Chase of the F.B. I."

First thing I found out was Chase was not me man's real name. And I was guessin' that maybe Robin A. Hood, the name on the credit card he'd paid for our room wasna neither. Nothin' makes a monster happier than a mystery I can tell you now. Meant there'd have to be a hunt. Sharpens the senses, makes the hunger grow. But, I dunno where to start up after that. All's I got left was to ask the general direction he took off in the jeep. That got me the gas station across the highway. And from there, I got a description of my blonde handsome FBI agent heading Northwest in his jeep. I put my thumb out and sparkled me whites for the next hour til a trucker stopped and took me on further.

We wound up on the edges of some big American city. He was gonna head South then but for farewell, we had some pints at a bar and later, I took enough drink to last me a while in a run-down hooker motel. I left him his wallet but took a few bills to keep me heeled. Before I left, I noticed I'd left some marks on his cock, chew marks like a dog with a bone. That was a first in a long long time. Me monster must be upset. I checked the trucker's pulse, though, and he was breathing. He'd live and I'd live and it was time to move on.

I walked into the big American city, hopin' desperately for some inspiration.

To be honest, I was at a bit of a loss. I had no real plan. No insight. I just wanted to get me man back. Maybe pay him back a little. Most definitely fuck him, that was a sure thing but the how to, the getting', the whole of it, I was baffled. Before the monster took over, I worked like normal fellas. Had me a job in a Baliff's office, doing accounts, had been thinkin' on going to University, maybe for accounts and records so I wouldna be passed up on raises by fellas with degrees. After the monster, I'd been a drifter, a hustler. I didna really know how to help me monster find me man.

So, I decided to call the credit card company and report me card stolen. Find out when someone used Robin A.

Hood's card last and their whereabouts. After all, I had relieved Chase of some of his wallet just a few days ago, yea? Lookin at me pocket full of licenses and credit cards, I found me Robin's SSN# along with Chris Edward's, and Jonah Woodsmith. I was charmin' with the gal on the phone and even though I'd forgotten me password and only had me social, she let me have the info. Bless her sweet trustin' American heart.

Woulda you believe that my luck'd changed for the better? Me card was being used right now at some strip joint. I flagged me a taxi and set off.

I was in love once. Even one like me can feel somethin' close to real human feelin's. I'm not a socio or psycho. I just have a wee fetish that can kill a body if I'm not careful-like. I fell for a Scots fella, Jamie McDonnaugh in London. It didna last but not from lack of me tryin'. It's just that way, I suppose: me hells last eternals, me heavens not so much.

I remember he had rough hands from tending pub, red, strong but the skin like sandpaper. He had a husky laugh, a barrel laugh, and a rough shadow beard he never coulda rid himself of. Red of hair, blue of eye, he was a Scotsman t'rough and t'rough. He was a good mate. Didna ask for anyt'ing. Took me in stride. Fella likes that, you know, being accepted for what he seems and all. Dont wana be changed. He didna know what I was for sure but he didna care neither. We had our good times and that's all we needed. I never drank from him. I didna want him mixed up in the darkness that's me.

I took me drinks from others: quick fucks in alleys, in bathrooms, in the dirty filth of the world. I kept our bed clean, our flat cleaner and not'in' of the depraved filth that was me ever touched me Jamie. Til the day it did.

I'd given these two a sandwich fuck in some skank hole for men. They were rough, I wouldna give them a second glance ot'erwise but they'd been tossing around bills all night at the pub, givin' up pints to all and any. They'd been flush with it and I wanted it. I wanted their wallets. And with their rough hard looks, I wanted some of that too. Jamie was too good for the likes of me, see. Too good and that made me feel bad at times. Made me wanna hurt him. Hurt me. Hurt us both. Only way outta that, find someones elses to take the pain and hurt out on.

So, I courted and charmed. Played up to them and we ended up in a dirty needle ridden room fuckin' like monkeys on heroin. I took their come, their blood, their money. I left them hallucinating, nearly dead from loss. I was that angry with meself, in that much hate of meself.

They repaid in full two weeks later, shootin' me in the chest and sweet good Jamie McDonnaugh in the head. I survived I guess. Jamie not so much. And I tried. I did. But once they've gone on to the ot'er side, there's no bringin' them back.

I see Jamie's face everytime I close me eyes.

I walked up behind him. It was a skank hole: dark and dismal, the women strippers run down and tired. He was sittin' up front of a middle stage, drinkin a tall glass of beer, his back to the door like a mark, not a smart copper. It was too easy. I sat down next to him and opened my mouth to say somethin' smart and he pushed a warmish glass of Guinness at me. He took a long swallow while I stared at the Guinness.

Then he said, "Took you long enough, Robin."

"You're a right charmin' bastard you are."

Chase nodded, not even lookin' aside to me. "That I am, Irish."

35

"Who the fuck are you then?"

Chase used his glass of beer to point towards mine, "You should drink that."

I looked at the Guinness. I gotta say, I've never met a Guinness I didna want. No harm in that, anyway. I drank and we said neither a word for a long time while a tired worn-out gal crawled on the stage in front of us, bills in her crotch and mouth.

Then, Chase said, "So, do you trust me, Lochlan?"

I nearly choked on me Guinness. I glared at him, wipin' me mouth with the back of me hand. "No, I dunna. After our drinks, I'm thinkin' on murderin' you, honestly."

Chase turned, looking off behind us a ways, and said, "Hmm."

A hand fell on me left shoulder. You know, there is only so much a man canna take. I slammed me Guinness on the table and jerked upwards. The hand shoved me back down again and squeezed me shoulder. Somethin' burned me so I glanced over. Silver bloody rings. Fat silver rings on fat hairy spider fingers. Bloody fuckin' hellfire. I turned the other way and saw the other fella. There were two of them: one thin in a suit, the other a gorilla with me in his paws.

"Is this him?" a tall thin dark man asked from behind us, his voice soft and nasal.

Chase drank from his glass leisurely, observing the beer in the light of the skank hole as if it were diamonds. "Yes," he said finally, nodding.

"Come along, Robin A. Hood," the larger man behind me growled.

I shot a quick 'wtf' look at Chase. Chase's eyes glistened with amusement.

The man jerked me up, my arm wrung behind me back and held tight in a silver ringed hand. His other meaty paw circled me neck and helped guide me. Wouldna you know it, we were headed for the lavatory. Beauty. Me entire life's been spent in the crapper. The gorilla steered me in and bellowed for two other fellas to get fuck out. He shoved me hard and when I turned back 'round, he hit and spun me again. A few of those and I came 'round on the floor, damp with piss, me needle teeth humming behind me canines, me own blood in me mouth and eyes.

They were all there, Chase and thin man and gorilla. Gorilla was polishin' up his knuckles for 'nother round while thin man kept repeatin' his words til I heard them and even then, I weren't sure I was hearin' them proper. "Where's the money, Robin? Boss wants the money back."

"Whah money?"

Gorilla came forward and hit me in the side of me bloody head. Saw me some stars I did. Monster howled inside, wanting out of his cage. Something slid across Chase's face. I knew then where the money was. Chase smiled cos he knew I'd seen him true. So tired I was bein' the butt of jokes. I said Go Monster, be free!

And he was. And I was.

When Gorilla came forward this time, I jumped up into him. His t'roat in me needle teeth and I jerked me head in kill bite. I held him tight and close and we hit the back wall. He tried to rip me away and I dug in deeper, tooth and nail. His fists t'undered on me head and back. Gorilla roared, angry at first, then panicked, frantic. I tore cartilage, muscle and sinew and drank deep: his blood, his voice, his very breath. His fists hit me then, slower, weaker and I growled a wolf's pleasure as his blood spurted into me t'roat. Not hadda real drink in so long, near forgot the intoxication. The power of it. Every life holds a song and even the death song of Gorillas is sweetest poetry.

Wetly, we slid down the wall and I raised me head to find me F. B. I man.

They were both starin' at me, thin man and Chase. I wiped me mouth with the back of me hand. Chase coolly took a gun out of his jacket and put it to the thin man's head. Gun went pop fzzzle. Thin man shot out sideways, dropping hard and sudden.

I rose up and when Chase backed up towards the door, I circled and trapped him. I took the gun from him and shoved him backwards. I put the gun in the back of me jeans. The door now at me back, I stepped forward, walkin' him, me head cocked sideways to regard him. Chase back pedaled back furt'er into the lavatory, his fine shoes slippin' on the blood and piss floor.

"I like you, Irish," Chase said, his hands up in surrender. "You keep your cool even when your balls are to the wall. It's a refreshing quality really."

"Izzit?"

"C'mon now. Tell you what, let's have a beer and a fuck on it. Cement our partnership. Contemplate our next adventure."

"I dunno. I'm thinkin' now's a good time for you to die."

Chase slipped, just catchin' himself. I leaned into him, now physically walkin' him backwards to the far wall.

"Really?" Chase said, tryin' to find the humor in it and failin' most miserably. "Really? It comes to this?"

I pressed meself into him and we hit the far wall. Chase pushed at me. I didna go anywhere. I'd said to me monster, Go! Be free! And he was, and it was too late to call him back into the cage. I honestly wouldna too sure I even wanted to. Chase was a most terrible man. His monster had betrayed me twice now. I think me monster wanted a turn or two.

Frater

Benji Bright

Teddy's face is streaked red, yet the sparkle of his green eyes comes through the grime, the gore. He smiles, and his blood-splashed lips pull away from white teeth. His chest heaves under his white tank top, nearly soaked through.

"You were *excellent*," Teddy says. When Leo doesn't match his joyous expression, Teddy downshifts to a self-satisfied grin and tries again. "We're getting better as a team, I think."

"After a dozen kills, I'd hope so," Leo says. He looks down at the body between them. It no longer resembles anything human. The veil has been lifted, torn to shreds. More mosquito than man, it whines as it dies; this is their fourth kill in a week.

"Weird how they wither, turn to dust. It's like their bodies suddenly remember that they were never supposed to be here," Teddy says.

Leo doesn't reply; he wipes his bloody hands on a towel and scans the room for evidence to destroy.

"Why aren't you happier?" Teddy asks. "We rid the world of another one."

Leo gives up on cleaning his hands for now. "Does an exterminator pop champagne every time he wipes out an ant colony?"

"Ant colony... nice." Teddy laughs, shakes his head, and nudges the corpse with his foot. "Well, that's *some* fucking ant. Christ, do you have to be so frosty? It's dead, we're not. Lady Luck gives me champagne; I'm gonna drink it." Teddy doesn't wait for the retort, he pulls off his backpack and starts taking out cleaning supplies. "Now, can we finish up and get out of here? If we hustle, we can still make last call at the Black Stag."

Teddy and Leo take a few hours to remove all traces of themselves from the creature's apartment. Leo deletes his profile from the app where he matched with the blood-eater and takes the creature's phone to do the same on the other end. It's obscene how easy it's become for the monsters to prey on the vulnerable, the lonely. Then again, it's also gotten easier for people like Leo and Teddy to find them.

And there's the matter of the weapons: a police-issue nightstick, a machete, and a taser. Teddy reaches for them—"I've got it"—and puts them into his pack. "I've got it." Neither of them needs to mention their respective odds of getting searched if campus security should become suspicious.

"Thanks," Leo says and tries to mirror Teddy's easy smile, but he can't seem to summon the levity.

The Black Stag is closed when they get there, but Wendy—the bartender—is a fan of Teddy, so she lets them in and pours them each a double vodka gimlet. Teddy looks suspicious as she slides the drinks across the freshly washed oak bar. He's not a vodka guy.

The whole place reeks of cleaning chemicals, and there's a strong similarity to the smell of the products they've used to clean up the scene of their recent kill. Leo's stomach shudders, but he sips his drink anyway.

Seeing their expressions, Wendy shrugs. "I capped the other booze already and was going to throw out the lime juice, so this is what you get for coming late. Where were you guys anyway?"

"Study session," Teddy says too quickly.

"You? With a book? I'd have to see to believe it." Wendy looks over at Leo and taps her own ear twice. "Got a little blood in your ear, Fight Club."

Leo reaches up, and his finger comes away wet.

Wendy shakes her head. "Keep your secrets. Just drink your drinks and go home. I need to mop the floor."

Wendy disappears, and Teddy takes out his phone. He's tracking another three or four potential blood-eaters. He doesn't ever stop; it's the thing Leo likes best about him.

"Tomorrow?" Leo asks.

Teddy shakes his head. "Nope. We've got plans, buddy. Points ceremony is tomorrow."

Leo rolls his eyes and Teddy frowns; it's unnatural for his perennially ebullient features. "I get it. You're too cool for school, but awarding points is a big part of all this."

"Why?" Leo asks. He can feel his hand on the wheel, pulling toward the crash, but he's powerless to stop it. "How does divvying up trophies make the world safer?"

The fight they're about to have is older than either of them: it's the schism between hunting for survival and hunting for the sake of the blood taste on the tip of your tongue. In a moment of clarity, Teddy decides that perhaps it's best not to rehash this particular argument.

"OK, fine, you win. It's all vanity and vapidity, but you—"

Teddy jabs a finger into Leo's chest and lowers his voice. "—agreed. Spearpoint didn't coerce you. You joined up, you got involved, we're *brothers* now, and this how things are done."

Leo opens his mouth to respond, but he realizes that the thing building inside him is too furious to be ejected in this closed bar. It would sear his throat, scar the air, incinerate the fragile thing between them to ash. Instead, he closes his lips and swallows his words.

On paper, Spearpoint is an athletic club with a focus on hand-to-hand combat techniques from antiquity. It's notoriously selective. It's not the Society for Creative Anachronism. It's not what it appears to be.

Its members are not chosen in the once-yearly tryouts where sophomores from the college cosplay in leathers and beat each other up with practice clubs. The invitees are scouted long before they set foot on campus.

Leo got invited the summer he turned fifteen.

On a scorching night, he'd cut down an alley between two high-rise tenements, accompanied by a chorus of hip-hop and reggaeton jockeying for position through the open windows of apartments on either side. The melange of music, heat, and distant sirens formed the backbone of Leo's understanding of what it meant to be a city dweller. He was deft and confident moving through a neighborhood that fit him like a second skin, but he wasn't safe. Safety was an illusion. It was a suburban concept, increasingly exorbitant, so luxurious that he and everyone he'd ever known had simply been priced out.

So when the figure slid away from the wall of the alley in front of him and moved to block his path, Leo was startled but not shocked.

"Hey, little man. Lemme talk to you," said the shadow.

The voice was too smooth and unaccented to belong to someone leisurely hanging out below 17th street in the middle of the summer night on a span of blocks notoriously hostile to outsiders. Leo's mind screamed danger, and he reached into his pocket and fingered the hilt of a hammer that was his constant companion after sunset. He tried to look casual, defenseless; it worked.

The thing wearing a man's face lunged. Leo's answer came so quickly that the creature's visage barely changed when the blunt edge of the hammer drove into the side of its head. The flesh wasn't as soft as Leo expected. Instead there was the hesitant yield of driving a shovel into hard earth. The force of the blow sent them tumbling toward the ground together like drunken lovers. The monster, dazed, attempted to extricate itself from the murderous embrace. Leo took advantage of its slowed reflexes and drew the hammer back to take another shot at the thing, which already seemed less human.

This blow was more vicious, more intentional, and caved half the thing's face in. It made a horrible, sickly whine as the metal did its uncomplicated work.

Leo staggered to his feet with the hammer loose between his fingers and tried to catch his breath. As he watched, the creature curled in on itself. It purpled like a man-sized bruise and then withered.

Whatever it really was, it had a long proboscis where its nose should've been and large, bulbous eyes. Leo watched it die and, in dying, shed its human skin.

He stood there for a long time before his hand stopped involuntarily clutching the hammer like a lifeline, and he was able to let it clatter to the ground. Eventually, he could again perceive the feel of the humid night on his skin, the sound of music, and the reassuring drone of distant cars, but it was hours before any of those noises rose over the sound of Leo's violent pulse driving in his ears.

He didn't tell anyone what happened. He kept the horror of it to himself, let the wound scab over and make him harder.

Two weeks later, the invitation arrived: a simple brown envelope within which was a letter sealed in wax and printed in a neat hand. The message was straightforward: an organization called Spearpoint had reviewed—and subsequently destroyed—the CCTV footage from the security cameras in the alley. It had taken them time to find the fifteen-year-old behind the unassisted eradication of a blood-eater. (*Blood-eater*, Leo thought, *not monster? Not vampire?*)

The letter outlined what might happen next: Spearpoint had chapters at several universities, and assuming that Leo could gain entry into any of them, he would gain immediate consideration as an initiate into the group. The murder he had committed was a crucible that few had met and marked him as one of them: a killer whose purpose was righteous, but a killer nonetheless.

Until the moment he read that letter, Leo had not considered the future, not really. He had not understood the future as a thing to be planned and hammered into shape. He assumed it would merely happen to him. Joining Spearpoint wasn't much of a decision, just momentum.

The points ceremony has some highbrow Latin name that Leo didn't bother to remember, and Teddy is always worried about his appearance. Leo's partner wears a light blue collared shirt, a darker blue jacket, brown loafers, and form-fitting khakis this time. He looks like he's been ripped from some cliché college brochure, but Leo finds his gaze traveling across Teddy's broad shoulders regardless.

Similarly, Teddy looks Leo up and down. "That's what you're wearing?"

"It's what I've got," Leo replies.

"I could loan you something...."

"Do you think I need it?"

Teddy takes a second lingering look. "No, no, no. You look fine. Let's go." His tone is light, but as they make their way, Teddy glances at Leo's polo shirt and scuffed shoes.

The two of them form a *cadre*, a singular hunting unit, so the actions of one reflect equally on both. Questions of personal style aside, they each attempt to be conscientious of this fact in their own ways.

When Leo and Teddy arrive at the ceremony, they are announced by their designation: Stinging Nettle. Teddy, as he usually does, winces at the introduction.

"Stinging Nettle. More annoying than deadly...."

"Shut up, Teddy," Leo whispers.

The Master of Ceremonies goes over the most recent kills. Only Sacred Cross (*Now there's a name*, Teddy opines) has committed more executions than Stinging Nettle for which they receive a commendation from Spearpoint's custodian: a positively ancient man whose affect is perpetually stuffy and whose oration is glacially slow. He talks about man's greatest enemy being his confidence in his safety when the world is infinitely more dangerous than he knows.

The custodian eventually comes to Teddy and Leo, congratulating them on a well-done job. He puts a hand on Leo's shoulder, stares at him with cloudy eyes, and says, "Excellent work, my boy. You're a credit to your people."

Leo attempts a smile, hoping it radiates the warmth he doesn't feel.

*

After the ceremony, they go back to Teddy's room. Leo sits on the queen-sized bed with its profusion of pillows and lush duvet, while Teddy loosens his tie and reaches for an open bottle of cheap gin.

"I have an open shift at the cafe in the morning," Leo warns.

Teddy squints. "Really? Shit. That sucks."

"Yeah, affording food and paying tuition *does* suck."

"Are we doing this again?" Teddy reaches for beer instead, warm to the touch, and throws one to Leo, who snatches the bottle out of the air.

Leo sighs. Teddy is a Spearpoint legacy and has a lineage behind him that means something when he enters a room of hunters. And he has money; it's the second blade that's always up his sleeve. "You're right," Leo says. "Let's leave it."

But Teddy doesn't slip back into his easygoing mood. Instead he stands on the other side of the room and folds his arms, sips his beer, and works something over in his mind as he stares at Leo.

"I'm not a fucking asshole, Leo," Teddy says eventually.

"Didn't say you were."

"So why are you treating me like one? Have I been less than welcoming to you?"

"We don't have to do this, Teddy ..."

"We do. We're a *cadre*. We're a fucking *team*." Teddy hesitates, questions how far he should go. "We're supposed to be brothers."

"We're not brothers."

"And that's my fault?" Teddy asks, clearly hurt.

Leo takes a long slow breath. "We're partners. Isn't that enough?"

"And fuck whatever I want in this situation?"

Leo feels the prickle of danger working its way up his spine, yet he asks, "What do you want?"

Despite its warmth, Teddy sips the beer. "More."

"You're an entitled shit, and you want me because you want everything. Because no one has ever told you no." The words are an arrow loosed: immediate, violent, and irretrievable.

Teddy doesn't recoil though. He takes another sip, then shrugs. "Maybe." He walks over to the foot of the bed and stands with a few inches between his knees and Leo's. The amber beer bottle dangles from his fingers. "But here we are, aren't we?"

"Here we are," Leo repeats as he reaches up and grazes Teddy's knuckles with his fingertips, letting his hand slide down around the neck of the bottle. Leo takes the half-empty beer from Teddy's hand and puts it his lips to drain it. "Maybe I want everything, too."

Teddy descends to the mattress and takes off his tie. Leo pulls off his polo shirt. When they come together for the first time, it's with a hesitancy that surprises Leo. During their hunts, there is no equivocating; each move is bold, swift, sure. They earned the admiration of their Spearpoint peers through speed and diligence, so this caution is new.

Leo has always imagined a young Teddy racing through the daughters of the one percent at whatever boarding school he graduated from and seducing sons during country club summers. These slow and gentle touches are a surprise. Perhaps there are different first times for every hunter.

Teddy is an excellent kisser, his tongue eager and playful against Leo's. Teddy's hands move up and down Leo's bared ribs, encouraged by the sounds they stir in Leo's throat. A hand drops down between Leo's thighs, and when it catches the warm pulse of Leo's hard dick under his chinos, Teddy grins but is already exploring elsewhere.

By contrast, Leo's attentions are almost ponderous, calculating the exact length of every kiss and planning when to break away. When he grabs Teddy's chin and tilts it back to expose his partner's throat, he can almost hear Teddy's moans a fraction of a second before they happen.

The rhythm they settle into is borne of compromise: Leo indulges Teddy's anxious need to quicken the pace—tweaking a nipple, another kiss, groping ass, a longer kiss; then Teddy leans back and lets Leo work on him with a carefulness that seems to generate its own gravity and brings the simmering, barbed eroticism between them to the fore.

"You have beautiful eyes," Teddy says, reaching up and cradling Leo's face in his hand.

"Thanks. Am I supposed to compliment you now?"

"It's customary."

Leo reaches down and works a finger inside Teddy's sweaty hole. "Your ass is tight as fuck."

Teddy rolls his eyes but can't hide the shiver that runs through him. "Can I ask you to fuck me? Is that weird?"

"It wasn't until you said that," Leo answers.

Leo enters his hunting partner from behind, and only a brief grunt announces him. He throws away his slow, methodical pace in favor of deep, relentless thrusts that have Teddy gasping and wildly jerking himself off.

"Whatever you do to me, I'm gonna' do back to you, asshole," Teddy says, his teeth gritted and the crown of his head producing a conspicuous amount of sweat.

But he never makes good on the threat. When Leo is on his back, and Teddy is inside him, the resultant sex is slow and careful. Teddy's green gaze meets Leo's dark-brown, so deep they might swallow the world.

"I could stare at you forever," Teddy says. His cock grows harder, and Leo makes a noise that's either assent or pure, unvarnished pleasure, though Leo doesn't clarify, and Teddy doesn't ask.

They flip and fuck until there are no more words, and it's nearly dawn. Leo slips out to work while Teddy sleeps.

The next blood-eater dies with Teddy holding it in a headlock while Leo drives a screwdriver into the equivalent of its heart. TThe two of them breathe hard as it struggles to escape them, trying to penetrate Leo's throat with its needled proboscis. Gradually, the fiend seizes and dies; they lower it to the ground.

"You seem lighter when you work," Teddy says after it's over.

"Yeah?" Leo asks.

"It's kind of sexy."

"You think everything's sexy."

"Nah, just you," Teddy says, grabbing for Leo's ass.

Leo dodges, but he's smiling when he says: "Stop fucking around, we've got work to do."

They clean viscera from their weapons, Leo's shoulders softening slightly, and Teddy's blood-splattered grin slick and full of glory.

Blood Ties

Cecilia Tan

Tim listened to his leather creak as he settled back against the bar and took a better look at the men around him. This was one of those nights when he could taste the smoke of the cigar-lover several feet away, smell the sweat and musky cologne of the man with his back to him, see each face clearly in the hazy dimness of the bar. The bottle was cool and damp in his hand, though he'd lost interest in the beer inside it. Every pore was open and aching for someone, something....

He hated nights like this sometimes, when he was alone, or he let himself feel sick about it. Too much like some nights in his childhood in the mountains, when he'd snuck out of his bed and run through the dark woods because he felt like he'd go crazy if he didn't, straining to reach something, touch something that was so needed but so far away. He'd always ended up crying alone in his bed, silently, so his father wouldn't hear. His father would have made some kind of religious pronouncement about it, Tim was sure, and sent him to the monastery up the road for "cleansing." But now

Tim thought he knew what it was he needed, what it was he had wanted all along: adulthood and the satisfaction that it brought, to be among other men like him, to touch and connect and be with someone else. Even if it was just to suck or get sucked off by a nameless stranger in a dark alley—some nights, that was enough. But tonight was one of the strong nights; he felt the tug and need deep in his gut and knew he wanted more: sex and power and pain.

The bar was beginning to fill up with men, the black leather creaking all around him. Somewhere here, there had to be a man who could handle Tim, or so Tim hoped. Some topman who could cage him and control him and fuck him silly all at once. More than once, he thought he saw a tall, dark fellow with a sleek ponytail looking at him, but every time he tried to make eye contact, the man had his head bent toward the surly blond boy next to him. *Wasting my time,* Tim thought. *He's already got one like me.*

Some hours later, though, Tim found himself still in the bar, frustration making him edgy and desperation turning him sour. He'd thought maybe that guy Mark would have been ready for another go. But he'd just laughed and walked away with a wave of his hand before Tim even had a chance to say hello. *Wimp,* Tim thought. *And I'd thought he had balls.* Maybe it was getting to be time to move on to a new city again, even though nothing terribly bad had happened here yet....

The blond boy was looking at him. Tim stared back in curiosity. The dark top was nowhere in sight now, and the boy looked a little lost. His hair curled slightly in front and his chest was well-shaped under his black harness. The boy started making his way through the crowd toward Tim. Tim met him halfway, by the pool table. The hard clack of one ball against another seemed to echo in his skull as he asked, "Why are you staring at me?"

The boy seemed younger now, younger even than Tim. "Because I, um, I saw you looking at me before...."

Tim pursed his lips as he listened to the boy's words and gleaned their underlying meaning: *fuck me, fuck me hard, I don't care if you're a top or a bottom, you're meaner and more experienced than me, and no other top would have me....*

Tim filled his chest with air, feeling as if the role of unwanted bottom had been lifted from him by this unexpected meeting. *Maybe this time nothing will go wrong,* he thought. It was easy to get the boy to agree to take him to his place, so Tim wouldn't have to explain his own lack of furniture, sex toys, or belongings. If the boy started thinking of Tim as the anonymous drifter he really was, he might back out. And now Tim wanted a piece of him.

The boy's place, a converted South End industrial loft, was as well-equipped as any dungeon or tack room Tim had seen in the three years since he'd discovered the leather scene. He rubbed his own erection through his jeans with his leather-covered palm in anticipation as he looked over the available toys.

"Put these on," he said, thrusting a set of leather cuffs at the boy. "Strip your clothes off first."

The boy's face turned surly, as it had been early in the evening. *No wonder his other top took off. Tired of this rebellious crap.* Tim, on the other hand, was beginning to wonder what it was like to break the will of somebody like that. What sort of methods could be justified? But surly as his eyes were, the boy stripped down to nothing and put the cuffs on his ankles and wrists.

With all his weight behind his shoulder, Tim knocked the boy to the floor. The boy looked up, shocked, maybe just a tinge of fear in his eyes. Good. Tim was much stronger than his size suggested. It had kept him alive on the streets many times in the years he had been vagabonding from city to city. *Now, let this pampered, prissy boy have a taste of that.*

He chained the boy's wrist cuffs together and hung them over the hook of a whipping post. Tim started snaking the belt out of the loops of his jeans. Yeah, some kind of bad boy/Daddy kind of thing...? He'd never done anything like that but he knew some guys got off on it. His own father had been a vegan and a pacifist—he'd never owned a leather belt, much less ever threatened Tim with it. Tim chuckled as he snapped the leather in the air and watched the boy flinch. His father had always said that eating red meat would make him a violent person. *Well, tonight I had a hamburger,* he thought as he let the belt fly. It raised a welt on the boy's left buttock and a cry from the boy's throat. *What would Dad think of me now?* With the rhythm of his arm swinging the belt and the regular wails from the boy, his thoughts drifted. His father had always talked crazy about some things; eating meat, sex, and violence were his top three. He'd been in bad shape near the end there, with raging fevers and delirium, his fears turned into twisted paranoia. But maybe it had always been paranoia, bad enough that after the accident that had killed Tim's mother, he'd moved away from the city and become a hermit with his toddler son. Tim just hadn't known it was paranoia until he'd gone out into the world.

He laughed to himself—maybe the old man had been right about sex and meat and violence all being one: the boy's back looked like hamburger now, with bright red places and mottled spots and bumps, and Tim wanted to fuck him. Tim tossed away the belt and shed his clothes, pressing his sweat-cooled skin against the hot, welted flesh.

His nails dug into the boy's chest as he pressed his hardness against the boy's buttocks, and his teeth grazed the boy's shoulder. He felt the boy stiffen as he teased him. *Let him think I won't put on a condom. Does that excite you, boy? To know you're helpless if that's what I want?*

The boy struggled to get away, but he was bound. Tim felt his lips part and the sweetly salty flesh of the boy's neck against his tongue. He began to suck, his teeth hard in his mouth, his erection hard against the boy's opening, his nails hard on the boy's skin... he was dimly aware that he had begun to shudder.

And then something sweeter than anything he had ever tasted began to flow into him, through his mouth and down into the empty place in his guts where he felt the longing, into his loins and out to the tips of his extremities. What he needed.... He tingled and surged and sucked harder and wondered why the boy was screaming what he was.

"Jeezuschrist, he's got me!"

So sweet. Tim felt as if he were slipping away into ecstasy, like that moment of orgasm, stretching on and on. Running through the woods on a cold, moonlit night, rarefied air burning in his lungs and his mind a million miles away...he could see the woods and feel the air. So long ago, and yet it seemed so real... another time, in the wind and the rain, the rain and branches lashing at his face as he made his way through the trees, racing the storm. The day of the visitors, the day his father had had visitors....

The boy was screaming now, and what he said made Tim wish he could stop and ask him how he knew....

"Argent! Argent!"

But he could not stop, could not pull away from the life in his mouth or the flesh in his hands, not until a hand grabbed him by the throat and forced him away.

*

Tim gasped as he felt the floor slam against his back. Where the fingers had touched his throat felt like fire, and everything seemed to glow around him. He looked up at the newcomer who was ablaze, or so his eyes told him, but even through the glow and flickering, he recognized the dark top from the bar. *It can't be,* Tim thought desperately. *It can't be Argent... some kind of a hallucination, the memory....*

This man did resemble the strange man who had come to visit his father when he was ill, his hair sleek and straight, his eyebrows thin and arched, but that was almost ten years ago, and this man seemed even younger.

"Timothy Delancey?" asked the dark man, who seemed impossibly tall now.

Oh god, Tim thought. *He knows who I am—he's a fed, tracked me across state lines, set me up with this...oh, fuck....*
"Look, it was an accident, okay?" That kid in Chicago had practically killed himself already, and that one in Columbus had been a mistake.... Tim had been sticking to bigger cities ever since then. Tim struggled to get up, to get to the door, but the man was on him now, holding him, keeping him from moving. His still-heightened senses felt the roughness of his clothes against his own bare skin, the rustle of it too loud as they struggled. Tim's head was buried in his own arms when the man said:

"Tim, don't you remember me?"

Tim stopped struggling while his mind raced to catch up. *This can't be....* "Ar- Argent?"

"Remember an evening full of rain and wind? The hurricane. I came in a red Jeep looking for your father. You were twelve years old...."

Another voice. "Jeezus, Argent, I'm bleeding here...."

"Shut up!" Argent hissed. Then, in a quieter voice, he went on. "I've been looking for you since that night, Tim. We've almost caught up to you a couple of times...."

Tim coughed as Argent let him go, and he unfolded halfway. Nothing was making sense. Why would they have been tracking him that long ago? He hadn't done anything yet. But had Argent been there that night in Columbus? In Chicago? "I didn't mean to kill them...."

Argent and the boy exchanged looks. Argent let the boy's arms down from the post and then knelt by Tim's side. "We know. We're here to help."

Tim saw the boy roll his eyes as he put a hand to the wound at his neck. Tim stabbed a finger toward him. "You got a problem?"

The boy snorted. "I ain't the one with the problem, boy."

Tim was on his feet, his hands reaching out to push the boy down again, put him in his place. "Who you calling boy?" But before he could reach, Argent was between them.

Argent's eyes went as cold as ice as he glared at the boy. "Luke," he said in a too-quiet voice, "why don't you go make us some tea."

Tim took a step back then as his mind wheeled. That was what Argent had said that night, as his father had sat and refused to listen to what Argent had to say and as Tim had listened in secret from the top of the second-floor stairs. Argent had sent Luke to make some tea.

This was the same Argent—the same Luke!—only Tim was twenty now, not twelve. The two looked younger than Tim remembered. "How...?"

Argent pulled his leather trenchcoat over Tim's shoulders. "I promise to explain everything. But you must trust me now—we don't have much time. How many times have you drunk human blood?"

Tim looked into Argent's dark eyes and watched the glowing halo like a corona around them. The chances of Argent being a cop seemed very remote now. "Twice before."

"Jeezuschrist," said Luke as he set down cups and saucers a few yards away on a cement table. "Third time is the charm."

"Then we're just in time," said Argent. "We're just in time." Argent gestured, and Luke brought him one of the teacups. Tim watched in frozen fascination as the dark man flicked open a small knife, made a slit in his wrist, and squeezed red out into the cup. He then handed the cup to Tim. Tim stared at the pattern of white lilies embossed around the edge of the cup.

"What am I supposed to..." but even as he was saying the words, he knew the answer and lifted the cup to his lips.

"Drink," Argent said. He folded his legs under him and sat on the floor. "Drink."

Tim poured the red fluid down his throat, slurping at the cup. Then he staggered.

"I suggest you sit, also."

Tim sat down hard, the cup slipping from his fingers as he pressed the heels of his hands to his eyes. The glow that had suffused Argent seemed to flare up behind his eyelids. He heard the cup shatter in a faraway place and Argent's voice—"Is it the visions?"—from even further away.

As the glow faded, images flowed and melded, the trees parted, and the roadway shone wet and slick in the oncoming headlights of a car. A Jeep pulled up to Tim, the window rolling down, and Argent's face inside.

Eight years ago, twelve-year-old Timothy Delancey climbed into the back of the Jeep, wet and shivering and desperate to know who this man was who knew his father's name, who wore a coat made of oiled leather and a tailored suit, who smelled like something pungent and sweet—an emissary from the outside world. Luke was there, too, in a similar suit, blond and silent.

Tim saw himself hidden at the top of the stairs, out of sight and straining to hear, listening to his father and Argent talk in riddles. They'd gone on for hours about things Tim could not understand well enough to remember, his father's breath getting weaker and more watery every time he spoke.

But then Argent had brought the subject around to Tim himself. "Does the boy know what he is?"

What am I?

"You're wrong. Timothy won't be that way."

"How can you be sure?"

"His mother was pure." *Pure what? Vegan pacifist?* Tim had never known his mother. He hoped they'd speak more about her, but they did not.

"But surely he needs his father's love?"

"Never. I'd never give it to him." Tim felt a chill. His father did love him, didn't he?

"If you don't, someone else will."

"You stay away from him, you pervert."

Argent's chuckle had been cold. "Oh, is that what you call us now? Very good."

"Yes, because you're sick, preying on...."

"Ah, ah...I prefer the term 'flirting'...."

Now, the chill crept up Tim's back. Was Argent dangerous?

"You *are* sick. You get anywhere near him, and I'll—"

"You'll what? Spout pacifist literature at me?"

"You can't touch him so long as I live."

"Which, from the looks of things, won't be long. John, that's why I'm here."

"You won't take Timothy away from me...."

"Calm down. I have no intention of taking him anywhere. I want him to grow up strong and healthy, just as you do. But you aren't going to live out the year."

"I'm stronger than I look—"

"Come on, John. We both know what it is that's killing you. If you want to live long enough to see Tim grow up, let me help you."

Tim. No one had ever called him Tim before.

"I don't see how you can help me."

"Kiss me, John. Kiss me and...." Tim began to back away from the stairs. He wanted to know, but he did not want to hear any more.

"No!" His father had begun coughing, struggling for breath.

"Kiss me the way you did long ago. Let my love heal you."

"Never again! Get away from me, you monster!"

The sound of a struggle. The sound of a cup shattering was the last thing he heard before he was out his bedroom window and out into the lashing wind and rain of the hurricane outside.

Tim found himself curled up, Argent's leather coat under him and Argent kneeling over him. He remembered looking at Argent in the bar, wanting and hoping that he might be the one.... Argent's voice was low in his ear: "What did you see? Tell me."

Tim felt the click in his mind as elements of his memory filtered into his present situation. He was naked and prostrate in front of this tall, dark man, a man who, he realized, he'd always associated with what was dark, forbidden, lustful, and dangerous. All from that one night's eavesdropping. The taste of blood was still on his lips, and his lust raged back through his loins. He shivered as Argent's hand came to rest on his shoulder. He wanted Argent to... to something. The smell of leather was in his nostrils, and his skin ached where he longed to be slapped and hurt. Tim never begged or asked for favors. He affected a surly look like Luke's. "Make me."

Argent squeezed his shoulder hard. "Don't play games with me, Tim. Tell me what you saw."

"Nothing, I didn't see nothing." He would not look into Argent's eyes.

He could see Luke's boots standing behind Argent. Luke's voice: "Are you sure this is him? Maybe he's just some kinky junkie, thinks this is a part of the scene."

"Tim, it's Argent. Remember me?"

Tim remembered coming back to the cabin dazed and dripping to find his sick father, Argent, and Luke gone. A few days later he had found his father's body near the house and buried it, and waited, but Argent had not returned. Tim shivered again as Argent's hand brushed his back. Maybe he could make Argent angry enough to whip him.

"Tell me what you saw, Tim."

"Make me," Tim repeated.

Argent shook his head and looked at Luke. Luke walked to the other side of the room and came back. Out of the corner of his eye, Tim could see Luke hand something over.

Tim's own belt. He watched as Argent doubled it over and tightened his grip on the end. "I've come here to teach you discipline, Tim. But I didn't think it would have to be like this."

Tim felt the first stroke of the belt across his back like an explosion inside his head, the pain setting off fireworks. Argent had that luminous look again, and Tim shut his eyes against the brightness, which seemed to be growing. Another stroke, and another. Tim struggled against the pain, even as he felt it surge through him like lightning, energizing him; he fought it until it overtook him, and he succumbed, letting the pain drive everything away from him, anguish, distress, disturbing thoughts...everything except for Argent, the source of it, the one thing left... it was almost as sweet as drinking his blood from a cup, and left Tim feeling a kind of thirst again.

Argent stopped and left Tim gasping. He looped the belt casually over Tim's shoulders. "Are you ready to tell me now?"

"Yes," Tim croaked, his eyes still clenched.

"What did you see?"

"I saw you...." How could he explain this? "I saw you in a Jeep in the rain...." He hugged himself and drew a shuddering breath. He couldn't say more, shame coloring his face and making him feel nauseous inside. How could he tell Argent that he'd been listening to that conversation?

Luke snorted. "That's as much as you told him, Argent. He's faking. The sonofabitch is just trying to get a kinky thrill out of us by playing along."

Argent shook his head. "Well, if it's a kinky thrill he's after, he's going to get it."

Tim looked up to see Argent slide his jacket from his shoulders and begin to unbutton his crisp, white shirt. It was hard not to want him—want his lean, sculpted body—as he stripped down to nothing. His cock had the same muscular grace, and it bobbed as Argent sat down again, cross-legged, and took a little knife out of his jacket pocket.

Tim gasped as Argent touched the blade to the crown of his own cock, then grabbed him by the hair and forced his head down onto the hardness there.

Tim let the erection slide deep as he began to drown in the sweetness again and lose himself in the images that swam before his eyes.

Like some kind of crazy dream, he could see his father across a low table, but somehow, he could also see through his father's eyes, Argent on the other side of the table. His father looked younger than Tim had ever seen him; Argent looked the same as ever. On the table, two small soup bowls, some chopsticks, stray grains of rice. Candles burned about the room, and Tim felt the weight of ritual in the air. Argent cut himself and let the blood flow from his hand into one of the bowls, and he began to speak.

"This is the only time we will ever speak of the blood or of the magic or of what we are in such terms. You must learn the way to speak of such things, so you will be able to pass among us and so we may work together, all without fear of discovery."

He could feel Argent's flesh inside him as he seemed to taste Argent's blood in the bowl, as his father took the bowl and drank from it.

"To speak of the bite is forbidden. To speak of the blood is forbidden. To speak of the hunt is forbidden. To speak of the kill is forbidden."

Tim heard his father's voice repeating these words and felt as if he were mouthing them, his mouth full of Argent.

And then the warmth became a spurt and another, and he swallowed eagerly as Argent came.

When Tim opened his eyes, Argent's were closed, and there was sweat on his brow. Luke stood a few yards behind, his face stony as he watched.

"Luke," Argent said. "Let me kiss you."

Luke did not move; his eyes flicked from Tim to Argent and back. Tim returned the stare.

Argent opened his eyes then. "Luke! I said I need you. Now."

Luke stepped forward with precise steps and knelt, hands crossed in front of him. Argent pulled him out of that careful stance as he pulled the wound Tim had made earlier to his mouth.

Now, it was Tim's turn to stare. When Argent pulled his mouth away from Luke's flesh, blood ran down his chin. He and Luke both seemed to glow. Luke sullenly put a hand over his neck again and sat back.

Argent's eyes burned at Tim. "Now tell me what you saw."

Tim shivered even though his skin felt like it was burning. Some kind of fever. His eyes locked with Luke's. There was some kind of challenge there, and Tim was eager to meet it. But he could not describe the crazy dream. He tried to recreate the words Argent had said, but he couldn't put them together. "The blood..." he managed, then put his hand over his mouth. Had he just taken an oath that said he would not speak of the blood? No, not him, his father, in the dream....

Tim looked at the two men across from him and narrowed his eyes. Argent got to his feet, his cock limp but long. "You're going to have to do better than that," he said, his voice dangerous and low.

"Yes, sir."

Luke yawned. "I'm telling you, this one's a waste of time. Remember that guy we tried in Buffalo?"

Argent gritted his teeth but did not take his eyes off Tim. "Third time is the charm. This should be causing his memories to bloom, but maybe John's brainwashing buried them more deeply than usual."

Luke got up and stretched and walked to where Tim's leather jacket had fallen. "Come on, Argent. Timothy Delancey had brown hair."

"Hair can be bleached. If this really is Timothy Delancey, then he's even more perfect than any of the others. John might have even done us a favor, isolating the boy that way...."

Tim wanted to back away, but he couldn't take his eyes off Argent's beautiful, cruel body. The beating had subdued the rebellion in him, and now he wanted Argent to push him, wanted to be taken. His breath came in shallow gasps…. Argent smelled pungent and sweet, and Tim felt small and young. *But can I trust him?* He reminded himself that Argent had possibly killed his father. Maybe this wasn't such a good idea.

Luke snorted. "I hate to burst your bubble, but his driver's license says his name is 'Roger Wilcox.'"

Argent turned to face Luke and took a few steps toward him. "What? Let me see that."

The cobra's eyes are off the bird, Tim thought as he backed silently toward the door. Before Argent could turn back around, Tim was down the stairs and into the alley.

Argent stared at the space Tim had occupied on the floor moments before. "Damn."

Luke stood next to him. "I'm telling you, once this kid figured out what our game was, he played along. He's just some hustler. But once he was found out, he split."

Argent shook his head. "But I was so sure this time." He went to the window and looked onto the quiet street. Luke came up behind him and laid his head on Argent's bare shoulder. Argent stroked his hair. "Get him back."

"What?"

"Go out there and get him back. I want to test your skills. If you have truly taken to the discipline, you will find him and bring him back to me without finishing him. If he's not Timothy Delancey, well, then you can have him when I'm done with him." Argent began to dress.

"Are you going out, too?"

"To flirt, to cruise," Argent said. "I need to score."

Luke narrowed his eyes. "That little creep didn't take that much out of you."

"No, but I'm going to need all my strength to prove or disprove who he is. And if I'm right, he's in a very dangerous position now. So get going!"

Tim felt like he couldn't walk in a straight line. He made it through the alley and across the next street. There wasn't far he could go, naked like this. He huddled in the barred entryway of the closed subway station where no one going by on the street would see him. He could fake like he'd been mugged. But he didn't like the idea of going to the police for help, even if it was unlikely that anyone had tied him to those two deaths.

If only he hadn't left his wallet and jacket behind. That drivers license had been helpful. He'd stolen the wallet off a trick in Providence because of the likeness. With his hair bleached, Tim could pass for the man in the photograph. Now, he'd have to start over again.

Or, he could go back to those two and ask for help. Now that he was away from them, Tim tried to think clearly. He'd run because it was his rule: run when things get too weird. It had kept him alive when he was twelve, he thought, and he was still alive today. Argent was definitely weird. All his talk of kissing and love didn't seem as strange to Tim now as it had when he was twelve, but the drinking blood and talk of a plan...there was just too much he didn't understand. Had Argent and his father been secret lovers before Tim's mother came along? Or...he replayed the conversation in the cabin in his mind. Was Argent his real father? Had John kidnapped him and hidden him away in a cabin to escape detection?

He couldn't make all the facts he knew fit together, but he couldn't just pick and choose the ones he liked.

Tim laughed, and his voice sounded too loud around him. Pretty far-fetched. It was an attractive idea, a nice fantasy to keep him warm on nights, imagining Argent was his father, beating him with a leather belt.

"There you are. Boy, you didn't get far." Luke looked down at the grimy nude form at the bottom of the steps.

"Get away from me," Tim said as he came into a defensive crouch.

"Look, we didn't mean to scare you. If you want to come back upstairs, I've still got your clothes." Luke came down the steps, his arms spread wide. Tim tried to hear Luke's real message under his words—he wanted Tim out of his hair badly. "Argent's gone out for a while. It's okay, really." Luke's smile showed white teeth in the street light.

"I just want my clothes back, and then I'll go."

"Okay."

"Bring them here."

Luke shook his head. "Bad idea. If the transit cops find you here, or worse, the Boston police, your ass will be fried." Luke took his own jacket off. "Here, quickly put this on, and come with me."

Tim took the jacket from the outstretched hand and wrapped it around his shoulders. Luke turned to go up the steps, and he followed. *Okay, I'll just get my stuff, and then I'll go. It was stupid to run out here, anyway. I should have just told them I wasn't really Tim Delancey, and they'd have let me go. I'd never see them again.*

They reached the vestibule of the loft, and Luke opened the door. Tim peered in. "See, Argent's gone. Here's your stuff."

Tim took three steps into the apartment, and Luke slammed the door and bolted it. As Tim turned to see his escape cut off, Luke body-checked him. Tim fell to the floor. Luke was on top of him before he could get back on his feet.

"You little shit, I owe you for this one. You've really got him in a tizzy, haven't you."

"I don't know what you're—"

"Shut up." Luke trapped Tim's hips by straddling him and backhanded him across the face. "You thought you were really hot shit, didn't you, first getting off on topping me, then as soon as *the* top came along, trying to bow to him. Well, you don't know what you've gotten yourself into, boy. Time for the payback." Luke bent Tim's head back and lowered his face toward Tim's throat.

Tim put his hands on Luke's chin, trying to keep him back. "Hey…you're the one who brought me home. Argent…."

"Leave Argent out of this, Roger. He's deluded, yeah, but he's mine. He's so into his quest for the perfect…man that he's convinced himself that you're some kid we've been chasing for ten years. So sad. Well, usually, he takes care of this part. But this time, it's going to be me."

Luke twisted one of Tim's arms and tried to bite Tim's wrist. Tim pulled his hands away and tried to hit Luke in the face. Luke caught his hands and held them together, trying to bend toward Tim's neck.

Why does Argent think I'm the perfect man? "But I am Timothy Delancey," he said. *Luke wouldn't hurt me if he knew Argent wanted me, would he?*

"Yeah, right." Luke sneered. "Well, I'm going to tell you a little secret, Roger. If you were Timothy Delancey, you'd be able to break this hold. You'd be able to do a lot more than lie there like a sack of junkie shit. Because Timothy Delancey, if he's even still alive, is a vampire."

Tim froze. *Okay, okay, okay,* he thought while he struggled with Luke, who was still trying to get his teeth sunk into his neck. His mind rearranged all the pieces and tried to make them fit again. *There's two possibilities here. One is, these bozos are totally fucking nuts, and it's this kind of crazy shit that my father tried to escape from. Two, he's telling the truth, and I'm a vampire.* Luke's mouth inched closer. But if they were nuts, how could they know that was his real name? And, if Luke was right, that Tim the vampire could get out of this, then that's who he must be. He strained against Luke again and held him off. "I am Timothy Delancey," he repeated.

"I don't care," Luke said. "I want you dead either way. It's the only way Argent and I will ever have any peace. He doesn't need you, and he'll see that."

"You don't have to kill me. I'll go away. You'll never see me again."

Luke laughed. "If you are Timothy Delancey, then I want you double dead. If you're not, then I just want you to feed my own strength. Argent never lets me have enough. It's always discipline, discipline, discipline. And he never lets me kiss... *drink* from him. But you've just had a taste of him, so if I have a taste of you..." He plunged suddenly toward Tim's throat.

Tim blocked his neck with the only thing he had left, his own head. Luke's teeth caught him on the cheek while Tim bit Luke on the chin. *Argent's blood,* he thought, trying to think of the sensations he had as Argent's blood had flowed into him. He felt a surge of strength in his midsection, which flowed out to his limbs...and he threw Luke off of him.

Luke snarled with rage and flew at him again. Tim rolled with him onto the floor, trying to come out on top. But they each threw fists in each other's faces and came away bruised as they separated. Tim bent his knees and waited for Luke to charge again.

This time, he let Luke bear him down, but he thrust his wrist into Luke's open mouth. Even as he felt Luke's teeth sink into his flesh, he had Luke's shoulder by the other arm and pulled his own mouth back to the wound he had made so long ago tonight.

Luke tried to pull away, but he was locked in the loop now, unable to stop feeding from Tim's wrist, even as Tim was draining him faster from the pulsing flow at his neck. Tim let his eyes close and let himself sink into that ecstasy once again.

A long time later, or so it seemed, Tim pried Luke's dead jaw off his wrist and rolled the body to the side. He sat up and drew a deep breath.

A key clicked in the lock at the door. Tim pulled his legs up to hide his nakedness somewhat and waited for Argent to come in.

Argent's eyes flowed over the scene, and he shook his head once. He took slow steps toward Tim, his boot heels tolling out a steady count. He went to one knee, took Tim's damaged wrist in his hand, looked at it, and let it fall. "Tim."

"Yes."

"I told him not to…ah well." Argent looked into Tim's eyes. "How do you feel?"

"A little dizzy. And everything is still all shimmery."

"It will be like that for a while."

Tim hesitated a moment before saying, "You killed my mother, didn't you."

Argent sat down on the floor next to Luke's body and said, "No."

"You killed her, and father fled from you, but you tracked us down in the boonies and killed him, too."

"No, no, no." Argent said. "To hell with the ritual. Let me start at the beginning. Do you know what you are?"

"A vampire."

"Yes. Now I'm going to tell you what that means. It isn't quite what you think. There's...power in the blood. Call it magic, call it sacrifice, call it an unexplained scientific phenomenon. Doesn't matter. When one human drinks another human's blood, power transfers. When one human drinks enough of another human's blood, it builds up. You become more powerful. You discover you can do things beyond normal abilities. You are faster, stronger, your senses are sharper, your reflexes faster. And you don't age as fast. Drink enough, and you stop aging altogether. But if you stop drinking then you begin to have problems. You degenerate. That's what happened to your father. And he was alive the last time I saw him, shaking his fist at me as I drove away."

Tim stared at Argent, knowing that what he was hearing was somehow true. His father had probably gone out that night looking for Tim, and the strain had been too much. "My father..." he said, but couldn't think of quite what to say.

Argent filled the silence. "He stopped drinking blood and tried to escape 'the curse,' as he called it when your mother died." Argent no longer looked at Tim but into the blank distance between them. "He killed her accidentally while they were making love. She never drank from him; he always drank a little from her. But in the heat of passion, he could not stop himself. He was... horrified, and rightly so. But instead of facing his difficulty, he ran off with you, swearing that you would never grow up to know the curse. If he had not been so stubborn—if he'd drunk a little from time to time to maintain himself—he might have lived long enough to see you grow up, and, who knows, he might have succeeded. Maybe if you had never tasted meat, you would never have discovered what he had. But I think you had the taint already, being of his seed produced while he was... active. And I think your experiences prove it."

The halo around Argent glowed brightly as Tim crossed his legs and put his hands on his knees. "But it was you who made my father a vampire."

Argent grimaced. "Not exactly. He had the taste already, but he didn't know what power it had when he started doing it. So many these days..." Argent's jaw was set in a determined line as he shook his head slowly from side to side. "In the old days, people were not so foolish and feared magic. There were taboos against drinking blood or eating flesh. But now..." His eyes went to the wall of hanging S/M gear, and he shrugged. "I tried to give your father the discipline necessary to contain the power, to use it wisely, but when he lost control with your mother...he fled as much from failure as from horror." Argent kicked at Luke's corpse. "And here is another failure." Then Argent's eyes seemed to focus on Tim for the first time since he had first come in.

"And you want to try it on me, next," Tim concluded. *The perfect man.*

"Yes."

"What do you...I have to do?"

"It involves intense physical and mental discipline. It involves invoking passions and controlling them."

Tim's eyes drifted to the array of bondage and S/M gear across the room and back to Argent's slim, strong, glowing form.

"If our power is to do any good for mankind, we must be able to control our appetites and choose to wield it wisely. That has been my function throughout the ages, training those like you, until they could go on to train others. But there are always those humans willing to risk everything to gain power, to misuse it. I'm hoping, Tim, that you'll join me."

Tim thought about life with Argent, and his memory of Argent strapping him across the back returned. He thought about bowing to Argent's will until his own will was shaped and formed and he could stand on his own. "I'll go with you on one condition," he said, one last piece of curiosity burning him. "You explain to me what you and my father talked about that day. Were you two lovers?"

Argent's smile was wan, his eyes betraying complex emotions. "I always wanted him, but no, we were not lovers. I was still trying to find the right paradigm for my disciplinary practices in the current age, and he did not want me. But as for what we spoke of, the kiss, love, flirting and cruising...." He broke off with a soft chuckle. "Maybe the ritual has its place after all. After this night, we will never again speak aloud of the blood, hunting for prey, or drinking. It is too dangerous. In the olden days, when people were more superstitious, we adapted the language so we could speak to one another about our common activity without detection even if we were overheard. In those days, men hunted for their meat, and so all our euphemisms and metaphors were of food. That rubric ceased to work in the modern age, and we had to find something else. Hence the bite has become the kiss, the blood, love, and to kill—"

"—to go all the way." Tim finished. "But can't that also get confusing?"

"What do you mean?"

"If one of us is your lover."

Argent licked his lip.

Tim wanted to curl up instinctively under that predatory look, but something in him also wanted to present his body to this man like a gift. He wondered if Argent could do the same trick he could, to hear what someone was really after no matter what they were actually saying. He'd always thought he was just smart, but maybe it was part of the magic. His tongue tumbled over the words "I mean, I want to be sure, if I ask you to fuck me, that you know I want you to... fuck me, and not...."

Argent stood up in one fluid motion. "I'll know." He stripped out of his clothes and herded Tim toward the heavy wrist restraints that Luke had worn earlier that night. As he strapped Tim's hands into them, he said. "After all, that's the key difference, isn't it? You won't make the same mistake your father made."

Tim shivered as he felt the belt brush his bare back. He would not beg, he thought, or ask for favors, but nor would he goad Argent into things. Luke had whined about not getting enough, but somehow, Tim was certain Luke had gotten exactly what he deserved. *I will be better than Luke, better than my father, better than all of them*, he thought, as the belt lashed at him like tree branches in a storm, like dark, wind-driven rain.

Darien Sucks

Jason Rubis

Lambert had long ago stopped wondering how the boys got into his apartment. It was enough that they were there almost every evening, waiting for him. Once the routine had established itself, he gave up on keeping late hours at the office and let his gym membership lapse. He all but ran home from the subway.

There were at least three of them most nights. The number varied, but the core group was always Sonny, Price, and a dark-skinned boy whose name Lambert never caught. They would be lying sprawled on his chairs and couch when he opened the door, playing his CDs and drinking his liquor. He used to feel a little pang of fear when the door opened, and he saw them there. It had eventually, like his curiosity about the boys' means of entry, simply stopped.

Most nights, Sonny would start them off. He would saunter over to Lambert, thumbs in belt, cigarette dangling (he always had a cigarette). Lambert would smile. He couldn't help it; his mouth always bowed in the same ridiculous, happy grin. Sonny just looked so *perfect*. A picture in a magazine. Sonny might strike him a light blow on the shoulder—a parody of camaraderie, only hard enough to send him stumbling back a step or two. Or he might slap his face, and that would hurt more; it would make tears jump in his eyes. But Sonny never went too far in that direction; he was always careful. Lambert appreciated that.

Sonny was tall, with a hard face and short black hair. His arms were scarred and strange with many tattoos, but his cock was long and uniformly pale and quite beautiful. He would take it out and point wordlessly at it, the cigarette jerking humorously in his mouth.

During all this, Price would be giggling. His big body always reeked of something sweet and earthy. Lambert never quite identified the smell—it was like pot, but it wasn't pot. Whatever it was obviously put Price in a playful mood. When Lambert got Sonny in his mouth, Price would shout for more liquor, food, or to change the television channel.. He would stomp. If Lambert tried to disengage himself so he could attend to Price, Sonny would slap his ears. When he went back to sucking, Price would come over and shout at him, kick him in the ass so that his head bumped forward, and it was a chore to keep the sucking pleasurable for Sonny. The dark boy rarely took part; he just lounged on the couch, watching the proceedings with a sleepy, beneficent smile.

Afterward, once Price had collapsed in red-faced giggles on the floor and Lambert was savoring the aftertaste of Sonny's cock, they might demand money—Lambert always made certain he had at least five fresh twenties in his wallet—and leave. On other nights, when the weather was bad (or, as Lambert liked to think, they were just perhaps feeling tender) they would stay a while. The three would take turns letting him suck them, then suffer him to lie naked and breathing and seeping on the floor at their feet. One might offer him a stroke. The dark boy sometimes got down and ran stubby, dirty nails along his back with the same indulgent smile he might wear if he were scratching a dog, and that was wordlessly delicious.

They would talk amongst themselves then. Their range of conversation was limited. It was all about new cars on the market or the girls they had recently fucked or a bouncer in such and such a club who was, quote, looking to get his motherfucking face rearranged, unquote.

Sometimes, they talked about Darien.

"Next time I see that bitch, swear to God, okay? I'm going to fuck him so hard, he sneezes my jizz the next two years, alright? Right? I'm going to *doom* that little cunt." Price never laughed when he talked about Darien. His beefy face grew red, and there was a focus in his eyes Lambert never saw any other time.

Once Lambert asked—shyly—who Darien was. Sonny drew unhurriedly on his cigarette. When he exhaled, words came out with the smoke, hot and biting.

"Darien sucks, man. He'd suck shit right out your pink little bunghole. Price?"

"Dude."

"D'you say Darien's a bigger pussy'n even Phyllis here?"

They called Lambert "Phyllis" when they called him anything because his Christian name was Philip. Lambert thought that was funny.

Price glowered. "Darien's like the pussy of the *world*, man. *Hate* that little prick."

"Not so loud, man," the dark boy whispered. Lambert saw the boys start, and their eyes twitch as one towards the wall. For the barest instant, Lambert saw them show fear. It was very strange, but it didn't last long, and afterward they were in a really terrible mood.

Lambert never asked about Darien after that.

One Tuesday night in August, Lambert found the apartment vacant. He waited patiently with the door open, but no one so much as knocked. It wasn't unheard of for the boys to stay away a night or two, or even several, but for some reason, their absence tonight made him nervous. Maybe they had gotten in some kind of trouble. Maybe they had grown tired of him. He spent the night in a nail-gnawing frenzy, too agitated to make himself a drink. He fell asleep on the couch, and when he woke at five the next morning, he was still alone.

They stayed away the next night and the night after that. The weekend was hell. Lambert grew resigned to their absence, but it left a hole in his life. He had few friends left in the city and had grown too used to the boys' company. Spending each night jerking off and watching television was driving him slowly crazy.

The escort agencies were the obvious answer but they proved disappointing. Lambert received a visit for two hundred dollars from a sleek leather-sheathed gym bunny who refused to touch him. Instead, the man invited him to masturbate while he flexed his muscles and dispensed pointed tips on nutrition. After that, Lambert swore off escort agencies.

Finally, reluctantly, he ventured out to the bars. He was looking for the boys, though he didn't admit this. He would stay slumped on his stool long enough to finish a drink, then go out to the alleys, where the trade congregated. But the alleys were always all but empty. He knew none of the boys now; they were ugly things anyway—hardly boys at all. All were on the wrong side of thirty and unappealingly paunchy. Still, the ritual brought some excitement back into his life, and through it, he rediscovered the pleasures of people-watching. Soon, he was closed out every place he went to. No one seemed very interested in him, but every now and then he managed to fall into a conversation, mostly with men his own age, and that satisfied him.

One night, two strange things happened.

The first happened on his way to the bar, which had recently become his favorite. His route took him down a side-street which was empty even at nine on a Saturday night. As he walked along, thinking of nothing in particular, he looked up at the side of an apartment building.

There was something *on* the building, next to a window near the topmost floor, a vague black shape flattened against the bricks. Even with the moon full and plenty of streetlights, Lambert couldn't figure out exactly what the shape was. Its strangeness vexed the eye, and he couldn't look away. Oddest of all, it seemed to be moving, creeping to the left, until it came to the edge of the building. Then it seemed to leap out, hanging in midair for a moment before disappearing around the building with a sudden, somehow emphatic jerk.

Lambert stood blinking for a while, then got on his way. It had been a strange experience, but not enough so as to make any lasting impression. He had forgotten about it in a matter of moments.

The second odd thing happened after he'd finished that night's drinking and, feeling nostalgic, ventured out into the alley. It was completely empty, but there was graffiti on the wall Lambert had not seen before: the words DARIEN

SUCKS, not in spray paint but lines of white chalk that had been scraped over and over into the stone so that the letters stood out with a kind of jagged ferocity.

"They sure do hate that Darien," a voice said, and Lambert started. An older gentleman was beside him, viewing the graffiti with impassive, somehow resigned eyes.

"Who?" Lambert asked.

"The boys. The ones that used to hang out back here, anyway. You'll notice there aren't a lot of 'em around anymore. That's his doing. Darien's. Selfish bitch." He laughed. He had a soft voice, so pleasant to the ear that his slurring was barely noticeable.

"I meant, who's Darien? Some friends of mine used to talk about him."

"Friends," the older gentleman said, with an insinuating smile.

"Yes, *friends*," Lambert snapped, flushing. "I'm talking about Darien. Who is he? Some pusher?" He felt proud of the effortless way he deployed the word.

"Pusher," the older gentleman said, stroking his stubbly chin. "You know, that's not a bad way to put it. He gives them things they think they want...things they think mean power, or, I don't know, freedom or what have you...but he's not giving, he's *selling*, it turns out, and at a higher price than they're prepared to pay. When he exacts that price... well. It's not pretty. Ugly ain't ever pretty."

"Does he ever go to the bars? Darien? Would I know him?" Lambert knew he was babbling; liquor had always had a way of making him chatty. "See, I think he may have hurt these friends of mine, and if he *did*...."

"Honey," the man said, touching Lambert's arm. "Don't. Just stop right there. Hurt your friends? He probably did. But there's nothing you can do about that. You can't *look* for

Darien. If he wants you, he'll find you. And you wouldn't be any too happy about that, chances are."

He turned and walked quickly away. Lambert thought about going after him; the man might be his only hope of finding the boys. But he knew he wasn't up to getting any answers from him, not in his current condition. The man would only laugh at him and keep walking, or maybe he would get frightened and call for help, and that would accomplish nothing. That, really, would be rather embarrassing.

So Lambert stood silently, staring at the graffiti. DARIEN SUCKS. He felt vaguely humiliated. He made up his mind that he would go looking for this Darien person the very next night. He'd go to every bar in the city until he found him. He wouldn't wimp out next time.

As it happened, the next time never came. As it turned out, the old gentleman was right. Because when Lambert got home half an hour later, Darien was belly-down on the couch. He had a CD on. Old Dolly Parton. He was moving his lips along with "Mule-Skinner Blues."

There was no question in Lambert's mind that this was Darien. He knew it with the drunken certainty one feels in dreams. But he would never have expected the terrible Darien to look like the man now occupying his couch.

Darien was a coquette gone to seed, his long blonde hair thinning around a visible bald spot. He looked only slightly younger than Lambert. He was no longer truly pretty, though the prettiness was still in him, still floating close to the surface and keeping his slightly too-long face appealing in an odd, sly way. Had Darien been less fortunate in the looks department, Lambert realized that if Darien had been less fortunate in the looks department, his face would have turned horsy by now. His outfit was too bright, too affectedly youthful to suit him. It showed off too much slack, tanned skin.

"Darien," Lambert said, then a shade less steadily, "You're him." He was in a slightly worse state now than he had left the bar. Vodka snuck up on you; he should have learned that years ago.

Darien turned his head so his cheek rested on one outstretched arm. Slowly he shut his eyes before opening them again. Lambert found this oddly unsettling.

"I'm him, okay. And you're Phyllis." Darien's voice wasn't the camp lisp Lambert had prepared for; it was soft and faintly country-sounding. It sounded infinitely tired. There was no challenge or threat in it, nothing like nastiness.

Lambert moved slowly into the apartment, shutting the door behind him. He took care not to get too close to the couch.

"What did you do with the boys?" His voice sounded ridiculous to him, raspy and squeaking. But he got the question out and felt immediately stronger for it.

"Nothing. I'm looking for them, is the truth. Or Sonny, rather. I got just mad as fire when the others ran out on me, but they ain't worth the looking. They're stupid, see. Stupid to the solid marrow. Their kind never really take to night jaunting. Not without Momma along playing teacher. Sooner or later they'll take a chance they shouldn't, if they ain't already. Then—*pfft*. But Sonny—he's smart. Smart enough to figure the dark paths without Momma's help. I figure he'll be back by here sooner or later. Mind if I keep you company while I wait?" Darien's eyes opened and shut again, and this time Lambert realized why he found the movement so uncomfortable to watch; except for this slow, somehow flirtatious winking, the pale blue eyes didn't blink. Not once.

He turned off the CD player but still hung back from the couch. He wasn't afraid of Darien, but the crazy talk made him nervous, in a way that was slowly eroding his lingering drunk. He pressed on even so, determined to get an answer before his courage evaporated completely.

"Who are you? The boys hate you. Everybody says so. They must have a reason."

Darien sat up suddenly, swinging his legs off the couch. He gave the cushion at his hip an inviting pat. His staring eyes seemed brighter now, as though he were noticing his host for the first time and found him rather interesting. Perhaps rather attractive.

"Why you want to bother yourself about all that now? That ain't nothing nice to talk about—bunch of silly little boys going out getting themselves hurt. Sit down here with me; let's us visit a little."

"No." Lambert was shaking all over.

"Aw, come on. Please? I'll tell you a story."

Darien's voice sounded wide awake now. It grew wheedling and honeyed and took on seductive cadences that disgusted Lambert. The man himself disgusted him. He was just an old simpering queen, the polar opposite of the boys' youth, strength, and beauty. Darien was nothing to be afraid of. Why the boys should so dread him was a mystery.

"You want a story? I know some good ones, hon. Back from the old days. There were more forests in the old days, you know that? That's where all the good stories come from. The forests."

He had some kind of hold on the boys. He was blackmailing them, maybe. Or maybe he really was a pusher. He gave them drugs and got them addicted so they would do anything he said.

"I'll tell you about the old Queens of Night and their brave and handsome consorts. I'll tell you the whole history of those pretty ladies, 'bout their warring with the daytime world and what came of that—how they forged the dark paths and set their children on them, forever wandering, forever devout, in thrall to the Red Secret."

Darien was leaning towards Lambert, reaching for him with a soft, imploring hand. His unblinking eyes were pathetically eager as he babbled on and on. Silly old bitch. Lambert could take his arm and twist it. Make him squeal. Yes. He could *make* Darien tell him where the boys were.

Instead, he took Darien's cheeks in both hands and kissed him. It surprised him how he did it—thoughtlessly, but with the surety of a long-held, long-suppressed desire. Darien's mouth opened under Lambert's, and Lambert felt his tongue working into the soft wet space, thrusting with a huge ferocity.

There was a smell. It seemed to explode in the room and had no one source, though it seemed particularly strong on Damien's breath and skin. It hit Lambert's nose first like the sweet scent that lingered around Price, then suddenly prismed into many other scents. Lambert smelled something like the mushroom smell of cock, the rich stink of too-long-unwashed jeans. A moment later, he was inhaling the salty smell of a locker room, the loamy stench of an ass well-fucked. It made his head spin and his cock strain at his trousers.

Memories flashed behind his eyes. Roland Marcos smirked and gave his crotch a contemptuous, surreptitious stroke as Lambert passed him in the dorm hallway. The taste of Alan Hess's balls and the sound of his laughter somewhere far overhead. Endless crushes, loves that never materialized. Magazine pages full of poses and heavy, laden balls, tender nipples, squirting cocks, pictures a much younger Philip Lambert had eaten visually until their every element was imprinted in his brain and guts.

There were other images, too, of many people and places he didn't recognize, but every one was about bodies and want and release. The shame these images might have once caused in Philip was gone now, barely a memory. They made him feel exultant, adoring, and adored.

It was quite marvelous.

And then suddenly, he was in Darien's arms, his head resting in his lap and being stroked. Darien looked—if not exactly younger, then infinitely more attractive, his little imperfections now charming. How was it Lambert had not noticed earlier how charming he was? His mouth was smeared with something dark and sticky-looking. Lambert chuckled. *She's smeared her lipstick.*

"That's right, sugar. You gonna do Momma good? Already have, haven't you? Yeah, you're a sweet little smackerel. A little taste of heaven. Might just have to keep you around a little longer."

Lambert grinned. He heard what Darien was saying, loud and clear. He was telling him how handsome he was, how strong and desirable, how utterly wonderful and worthy of love. It made a fierce joy in Lambert, so strong he felt the sting of tears.

Behind them, somewhere, a door was opening. No, not a door, but a window. A window sliding open. And there was a voice somewhere in the vicinity of the window, on the wrong side of it. A tiny piping ghost voice wailing a song of loss and jealousy. It didn't sound much like Sonny at all.

Darien purred. "Aw, well now. Little birdie's come home to roost. You excuse me a minute, sugar? Momma got to go put little birdie in his cage. For good this time. Momma'll be right back. Don't you go nowhere now."

Lambert sighed as Darien slid from underneath him. He relaxed on the couch as soft sounds filled the room:

hisses, cajolings, whispers, and weeping. Once, there was a bright, sharp noise like glass breaking. Once, he heard something irresistibly like the beating of enormous wings. And somewhere—in one of the other apartments, maybe— someone was watching a movie in which many people screamed in desperation and unending horror. Lambert paid none of this any attention.

Darien would be back soon. His sweet Darien would stay with him forever and show him how strong he really was.

He had never in his life, not once, ever felt so strong.

You Can Go
Your Own Way

John T. Fuller

This doesn't happen to him. Not to men like him. Things like this don't happen to men like him.

"Buy you a drink, mate?"

Matt swivels his eyes towards the voice at his right shoulder because moving his head seems like a substantial waste of effort. There are few reasons that a stranger offers to buy you a drink, and none of them are, in Matt's experience, savoury. The speaker is out of his peripheral vision, but he can see hands on the bar top; clean, young, the fingernails neat. It's unusual enough to merit turning his head to the side; by the time Matt does so, the man is already taking a seat next to him, and it's too late to nip this conversation in the bud.

"Busy tonight, hey?" the stranger continues, his *beat* a trifle too *up*. Matt regards him. He doesn't know or recognise him at least—mid-twenties, with the kind of 'effortless' cool that comes with a tourist price tag, the collar turned up on his leather jacket. Perhaps a fan of his writing, except he doesn't look the sort—especially compared to the other patrons in this hellhole stylie bar. Matt lifts one shoulder in what's almost a half-arsed shrug. *I come here because it's the closest place that'll serve me; I try not to notice how jam-packed with twats it is.* The man nods as if Matt's actually said something and he's responding. Dear god. So, not a fan, and thank fuck not trying to pick him up for some toilet action— too young for that and far too... attractive? Where did that come from? Matt closes his eyes briefly in self-disgust. The guy's probably some sort of con man, or—"Reminds me of back in the day," the stranger continues conversationally, and Matt thinks, *back where? Playschool?* followed by *Oh god, that's it—he wants somebody to talk at.* A brief glance around the bar reveals Matt as the only person sitting alone, never mind the only person not dressed in fucking harem pants—he's the obvious target. He sighs. "So go on, what's your poison?" his potential therapy client insists.

Well—a drink is a drink.

"Bitter."

"That a drink request or your state of mind?" The man smiles, flashing dazzling straight teeth. Great: a fucking comedian. Matt grimaces, and the guy's face drops back to neutral as he hands Matt his pint. His voice is quieter, less jovial when he says, "Name's Chant. And you are?" Thankfully, he doesn't offer a handshake.

Matt tries to avoid his eyes and mutters, "Thanks," and takes a long draught of beer, but he can feel those green eyes on him, awaiting his response. He can't not give it; it feels trapped inside like soda fizz. "Matt."

"Good to meet you, Matt." He's Northern, by his accent. Nobody is ever really from London, den of strays and immigrants and fuck-ups that it is. The sustained sincerity in his tone catches Matt by surprise, and when he glances up, Chant's eyes are still on him, and he accidentally meets them. Matt tries to hide his nose in his pint, swallowing almost half in one go. "Thirsty," the man says, more dreamily than such an observation—should such an observation ever be casually made—has right to be, and Matt can feel his own eyes go round with disconcertion as he goes back for a second attempt at crawling into his glass.

He's not used to being stared at like this. When he glances back at Chant, the guy does have the decency to look a little abashed, letting out a soft laugh and lowering his thick eyelashes. "Sorry, I—I'm not much one for socialising." *I find that somewhat hard to believe,* Matt thinks, but he curls his upper lip and offers a concessionary nod. *Now I, on the other hand....* The young man, sipping his beer and looking at Matt again over the rim of his pint glass, says, "I don't normally do this...I mean...." another laugh, shy eyes averted—he seems flustered, and Matt's stomach plummets, "it's been a while since I...."

Oh, hell no.

Matt doesn't answer but can feel his own frozen expression, and then he can feel it thaw under the heat of his companion's uncertainty and... embarrassment? *What's this? For once, he has the upper hand in a situation? Then just walk away, Matt, walk away.* But his wariness is giving way to vanity lubricated by booze, and why shouldn't some gorgeous young man take a fancy to him? He is, after all, not too hard on the eyes, his novels have a cult following, and he—wait, *gorgeous?* Matt sneaks another look again to check, just in time to see his admirer lick his lips, wet pink tongue darting like Matt's the most desirable thing he's ever laid eyes on. Matt's dick stirs; he fidgets on the bar stool.

Draining his pint, he finds himself slowly licking the beer foam from his whiskers in response; he can't help it. Chant's gaze hovers on his mouth, his throat. He says, "You want to go somewhere else? For another drink?"

Matt nods.

"I know a shortcut."

Chant follows the guy, weaving a little, down a side street that's barely more than an alleyway, disappearing into shadow between two parades of bars. TThere's a light at the other end of the tunnel, which means it presumably does emerge onto the next street parallel, but all the same, this is too easy, too easy… his mouth fills with spit, and he quickens his pace. The man, Matt, drops his chin to his chest and avoids Chant's eyes.

When Chant had first walked into the bar that evening, battling a noisy tide of young revellers—loud in volume and appearance—Matt had stood out as clear as the only soldier with his head above the trench. In a room full of fast-forward, Matt may as well have been on constant, jarring pause, the desperation simmering off him in waves, and Chant had thought: this man is begging to die. Chant glances over at him, Matt's head down and striding unsteadily with a kind of grim determination towards the darkest point of the alley. He's so obviously trying not to make eye contact. Maybe he can tell. It's sad, really: the guy's a bit scruffy, definitely pissed, probably alcoholic, and certainly depressed, but he's also clearly not a hopeless case. Not particularly old or even ugly—even if he's got no family, no mates, no reason he shouldn't find himself a nice girl to give him a reason to live. Or a nice guy…Matt slows and half turns, and the hunger-pang twist in Chant's guts gives him a twinge of guilt. *This is why you should stop thinking of them like they're people, damn it. This is practically a mercy-killing.*

"Alright?"

Matt doesn't answer, but he raises his eyebrows and sort of nods, baring his teeth in a grimace of a forced smile that reveals canines that give Chant another kind of lurch inside, a residue of pity or maybe empathy. Matt sways to a halt and steadies himself against the wall with one hand. He's tall—although Chant's quite used to people being taller than him—and he's broad, and for a second Chant doubts the wisdom of his choice, but it's clear the man's in no shape to fight back. As Chant closes in, Matt slumps, his shoulder connecting heavily with the wall, his whole frame sagging. He looks at Chant through a curtain of unwashed curls, his eyes pleading. It makes Chant want to say something; an apology, some comforting platitude, a pat on the arm *there, there—almost over.* Instead, he takes a step closer, his fingers curling around the sheepskin collar of Matt's coat as if to steady him. He tries to keep it unthreatening, but Matt doesn't seem in the least bit panicked anyway, lids sliding half shut over glazed eyes. Angling his head slightly, Chant leans up, and when Matt suddenly leans down too, pressing his lips against Chant's, for a moment, Chant is far too stunned to do anything but go with it.

Oh. Well, that does explain a few things. Then, *crap, this makes things a whole hell of a lot trickier,* and then *at least he's a good kisser.* By the time the few seconds have passed necessary for Chant to process what's occurring, he realises that he's still kissing the man back, and it's not unpleasant. It's been a good few years, decades maybe since Chant was with a man, and this guy is clearly crazy for it. Only kind to give him a nice send-off, really, it's what he would—evidently does—want.

"You're so…" Matt snatches words that Chant can't quite make out between breaths; he isn't sure they're words. Chant reaches up, twists the ends of the man's limp curls around his fingers, and lets his fingertips brush the nape of his neck. He skates across hot skin to seek the piston thud of his jugular pulse. Matt moans at precisely the same moment as Chant but for, Chant suspects, an entirely different reason. His mouth is open and eager and so soft, rankly sweet with the alcohol that's evidently now coursing around his bloodstream. Chant could get so drunk off him… he catches the man's lower lip gently between his front teeth, lets it go again, and feels Matt rock the hard bulge in his jeans desperately against Chant's hip. It would be so easy. The man's entire body is a freight train shudder—then, abruptly, he drops to his knees and starts tugging at Chant's belt, crouched like prayer, like last rites, in the dirt of the alley.

It would be so easy. Matt's scrambling fingers brush his hard-on, and Chant groans, thinking, *just let him*. He's not even sure where the hunger ends and the lust begins, but draining someone dry after they've just, well, drained you dry seems a little… impolite. He reaches down to pull Matt up to standing again, Matt frowning and swaying, and his eyes look so clouded with confusion that Chant says, "I want you here. Up here. I mean…" and he stops his words with another kiss so he doesn't have to try and explain, his hands wandering to the waistband of Matt's jeans. Poor bastard. May as well let him go out with a bang. The way he's whimpering, it's probably not going to last long. The heartbeat Chant no longer has, thumping like a snared rabbit; it's enough to drive him crazy. He touches skin, and Matt shivers, a full body shiver like he's coming already. Heat beneath his palms; pounding blood rising to just below the surface, suffusing and flushing Matt's skin, warmth coming off him in dizzy waves. Chant can smell it, that rich meat scent and he has to restrain himself from taking, from driving hard in, falling to and devouring. This needs to be gentle, a last clandestine thrill before death. Matt's toasted, but he's evidently not going to stay passive, tugging open Chant's fly in turn and that shiver again like he's never touched a guy before—maybe he hasn't. First and last. Matt's face is buried in Chant's hair, his hand working him with more expertise than expected. When Chant nudges in beneath his chin, lips to Matt's throat, Matt quickens his pace and shifts, whispering something. And then there's the hot scratch of stubble beneath Chant's tongue, guarding a pounding pulse that drags vitality thundering beneath that placid, pallid skin—the lava beneath the surface, waiting to erupt. He nips gently, rolling the flesh between his teeth, and Matt whines, pushing harder into Chant's fist. His skin is salt sweet, taut but yielding. As Matt gasps and Chant feels the warm spill over his hand, Chant penetrates smoothly, and when Matt tries to jerk away, he only pulls him closer.

Matt is down on his knees in a back alley and is entirely past caring. So what if he wants this? Lots of people experiment; hell, maybe he is gay—so big, fat what? He flicks a glance upwards and swallows the dryness in his mouth again. This stranger is beautiful, and Matt can just tell he's different somehow, and judging from how shy he was when he leaned in to kiss him, Matt will have to make the moves here. It's satisfying being in charge for once, so when Chant's fingers curl around his coat collar again, pulling him back to his feet, Matt wonders what awful faux pas he's committed. But he needn't worry. "I want you. Here. Up here." *Oh shit*, Matt thinks, as the man's tongue is thrust between his lips again like he just can't get enough, and the man's hands start to work at unzipping his jeans, *does he want me to fuck him?* He's spun for a second in that delicious epiphany until Chant's fingertips brush his dick, and Matt is jolted back to his beer-muddled senses; Chant's hands are *freezing*. It's the strangest sensation—the contrast between the pleasure of what Chant is doing and the almost-discomfort of cold flesh is maddening. He's not as cold elsewhere, but when Matt slips a hand down his pants, the flat plane of Chant's belly is still chill enough to make Matt shiver. He doesn't stay cold for long, though. His cock in Matt's fist is hot, and Matt buries his face in his hair so he doesn't have to look, breathes in the faintly furniture-polish-y smell of some trendy blokes' hair product, and marvels at how natural this feels. Chant's hand on his cock. Chant's lips on his throat. Maybe this is what he's been missing.... This man, stroking him closer and closer, maybe they'll swap numbers, maybe they'll meet up for a pint, oh god, he's so close now, maybe they'll move in together and live happily ever—

—*shit oh god oh shit what the fuck?* Matt's coming deliriously hard, the exquisite pleasure that's almost pain until he realises that, oh, fuck, it *is* pain—searing pain in his throat. He feels, simultaneously, the warm wet in Chant's hand still limply cradling him and the warm wet spill running into his collar beneath Chant's greedy mouth. He panics and tries to pull away, but his legs are weak from drink and pleasure, and now his head is spinning with agony and rapid blood loss, and. Matt feels a third warm wet of tears between his screwed-up eyelids.

It's not fair.

Matt doesn't even know why he's surprised. *Of course,* who would be interested in him except some pervert psychopath wannabe vampire killer? Things like this don't happen to men like him. Except, they do. They always do. At least, Matt thinks, as he sags in the man's arms, he is handsome.

It's a moment until Chant can even pause. It's always like that, too good, too far between. The sweet, alcohol-laced spill into his mouth; he could exhaust this man without coming up for air. When he slows and paces himself with a lick across the running wound, Matt is already heavy in his arms, his eyes darting feverishly behind delicate closed lids, like he's dreaming but fighting sleep. He's near the end, and his cheeks are wet; sometimes they cry, and Chant feels momentarily terrible. Frowning, he smooths a curl back from Matt's forehead, and Matt murmurs something, a moan of thwarted desire. A trickle of blood leaks, sluggish now, down his neck, and as Chant follows its trail with his tongue, Matt whispers, "No."

It's a lame protest, full of such palpable disappointment, such defeat. Such unwilling acceptance Chant thinks, but under it all, Matt's still alive, still struggling, and his weak pulse protests *no—not again.*

He tries to lean Matt against the alley wall, to leave him there—maybe he'll recover, although Chant knows he won't—but it's obvious Matt's legs will no longer support his weight. Another one, dying. He should just drop him and run, but there's something.... Chant feels bad. He feels more than the usual guilt: pity and something else. He likes this man. Matt's legs fold too easily beneath him, and Chant settles him on the alley floor with his back leaning half against the wall, half against Chant's shoulder as he crouches next to him. When Chant fastens his mouth again to the ragged punctures in Matt's throat, the man can barely raise a whimper. His once thundering heartbeat is as weak as moths. On its point of failing, Chant raises his own wrist and bites a tar-black gash that he presses to Matt's slack mouth, and this time Matt doesn't have the strength to try to pull away.

It must be a good few hours until the strip of sky overhead has gone properly dark, and Chant's feet are so stiff from sitting motionless on concrete with Matt's head cradled in his lap that he can't feel them. He's started to nod off when Matt stirs. They must look a sight, blood stained and bundled up—two post-fight drunks, people would think.

Chant says, "You awake? Alright?"

Matt grunts, hand reaching for his head: a hangover on top of the hell of transformation; that must be a fun one. Chant shifts, trying to wriggle some feeling back into his numb legs, Matt a dead weight on top of him. *Dead weight.* He cringes. "Do you... do you know what just happened?" When Matt looks at him, it's with new eyes. Oh, he knows. If he didn't fully understand before, if he thought he'd just been attacked by some nutter with filed teeth, he knows now. He feels it. The familiar sickness wells in Chant's chest that he's done the wrong thing entirely, saving this man out of pity and guilt, damning him to this life-outside-life. "I've got to go. You'll be fine. There're others, they'll find you. They'll look out for you."

"Stay." Matt's voice sounds torn. Like he badly needs a drink. Maybe it *is* just a hangover, Chant thinks, but he knows it's not. It's the reflex of fear, the habit of being scared of the unknown. The residue of his past life clinging.

"No. I can't stay; you've got to go your own way." He mentally curses his wording, and the song starts up stupidly and inappropriately in his head. He just wants to run. "What will you do?" Matt looks blank, perhaps about to cry. Then, that familiar dawning of realisation and sensation: the hunger, rolling like clouds across his face and bringing with it a smile vindictive and merciless.

"Atta boy," says Chant, with only a hint of wistful regret creeping into his voice. "You go get 'em."

He watches as Matt hand-walks himself back up the wall, staggering to his feet, and gaining his balance. He presses a palm to his neck and looks at it curiously when it comes back dry, the tear in his throat closed. Raising his eyebrows, he nods at Chant, then he turns and walks back down the alleyway without looking back, his pace picking up to an effortless jog as he rounds the corner onto the main street. Chant watches him go. He wipes his eyes with the back of one hand. And then he walks the other way.

The Vampyre's' Heir

Maxwell I. Gold

On some ageless night, I encountered that creature, which was both the most beautiful and deadly, my dearest Ruthven. Where the ghoulish dark and dreary fogs of eldritch hills painted an ancient landscape, nothing mattered when clutched in his embrace. Despite the knowledge of the sinister truth of his being, I wanted nothing more than to remain at his side. My sweet, his glance cut through me with a primal derision and force, unimaginable, as if I were swallowed by his eyes, lost in the sumptuous, heavy toxicity of his presence.

My body felt heavy, and the world around me blurred and opaque, where the only true forms I was able to discern were Ruthven's tall, slim physique. Drunk and stupefied on thick lust and fêted languor, the heaviness on my limbs grew more intense in a wild, pleasurable sensation as I looked up into Ruthven's eyes. Doing everything in my power, there was nothing more I could do as his cold, supple lips grazed my own where all at once, a flood of terror, ecstasy, and pain washed in fiery heat throughout my body. It was over as quickly as it began, where on some ageless night, I encountered that creature, which was both the most beautiful and deadly, my dearest Ruthven.

When Michael Comes

Whitt Pond

Night has fallen, and Michael is here. I feel him waiting outside in the storm, confused and frightened like a lost child in a strange place. It has been ten nights since he last left. Setting my book aside, I hurry to find him.

Tonight, he's on the roof, tapping frantically on the skylight glass, a pale figure peering in through the rain, his long dark hair wind-plastered across wet skin. He knows not what place this is nor what instinct has brought him here, yet in his face, I see the anxiety, the fear that perhaps no one will bid him enter, or worse, that no one will be here at all.

Then he sees me. He frowns in puzzlement, staring through the rain-streaked glass at a face familiar yet grown strange. And in the faint reflection between us, I see the face, too. I smile sadly at another bit of legend gotten wrong. It is not Michael who fears the mirror.

"Michael," I say his name softly as I unlatch the window, opening the house to the night. It is all the invitation he needs.

He enters, naked and dripping across the layered rugs, eyes child-like yet darkly dangerous as he scans the room. I close the window, wondering what happens to the clothes I give him. And resign myself to not knowing or really even wanting to know. I do not care. He is here.

I watch him in silence as he moves about the room, graceful in his uncertainty. He pauses at the familiar, wariness slowly giving way to fragments of memory as he touches a polished brass bedpost. An easel. Drawing charcoals and sketch pads half-filled. A framed photo.

His pale slender fingers, artist's fingers, linger on the last. The photo is old, but the faces are young and of an age with each other. He looks back at me, trying again to see the face within, and I nod. A name half-forms on his lips, and I nod again.

"Yes, Michael. It's me. You... you're home again."

I ache at the sight of him standing before me, tall and slender and naked in his bone-white need. He absently brushes his hair out of his face as his eyes, so exotic even in life, flicker with echoes of things remembered. It comes quicker now, the remembering. Or at least it seems to. The clock on the mantel chimes slowly in odd accompaniment to Michael's steps as he draws nearer. He pays it no notice.

Cocking his head left, then right, he tries to puzzle me out. Finally, he touches my face, his cool fingers once again seeking the familiar. As always, he is surprised by my warmth.

Slowly, carefully, I take his hand in mind. His eyes narrow with uncertainty, but he does not pull away. Even cold as his flesh is, I have to fight the urge to draw his body to mine.

"Come," I say softly, nodding toward the doorway. "You need...food...something warm.... Come."

He hesitates a moment, glancing back at the window and the night. Then he follows. His feet make no sound as we walk down the stairs. I think of Orpheus and do not look back.

In the kitchen, I set the warming bowl for body level. In a different life, we used it to heat the sake. I take one of the special bottles from the back of the fridge and immerse it in the rapidly heating water. A memory touches my lips, of hot sake dripping from his mouth to mine.

As the bottle warms, Michael wanders through the house in ghostlike silence, trying to remember. I manage to slip a bathrobe on him as he stares in puzzlement at unfamiliar rooms filled with two decades of post-Michael accumulations. He turns to me, the question on his face.

"It's a different place, hon." I pull the robe closed, lingering on the sight of his smooth chest, longing to kiss and lick him there. "You were never here. Not...before, anyways."

He listens, as always. I am never sure if he understands. Later, he does. But at this point, I'm never sure. I lead him to the living room, where bottle and bowl are waiting on the coffee table, along with a single porcelain cup.

Outside, the storm has settled into a slow, even rain. Michael stares out into the darkness, thinking what I cannot know. I open the bottle, careful not to spill a drop of what comes so precious.

The barest scent is enough. Michael turns, his dark eyes gleaming as the hunger suddenly comes to the fore, and quicker than the eye can follow he's at my side. I fill the cup not quite to the brim and then offer it to him. In spite of his need, he hesitates.

"Go on, Michael." I push the warm cup into his hands. "It's okay. It's mine. Go on."

He takes the cup, cautiously sniffing it. The aroma is heady, even for me, yet his fangs do not emerge. Not yet. He sniffs again, this time in indulgence, closing his eyes as he savors the moment. Then, he drinks and is lost in ecstasy.

I watch, almost in envy, as he feels the warm life flowing down his throat. The redness lingers a moment on his lips before his tongue licks it away ever so slowly with sensual thoroughness.

He drinks again, and I am drawn into his moment by the thought of my blood flowing into his body, filling him with life. My cock begins to swell with another thought, another kind of filling with another kind of life. I refill his cup and savor my own desires.

Even in the dim light, I can see the change occurring. His skin is no longer the bone white of delicate china but the slight tan of summer remembered. And in his eyes, the light of memory begins to burn with awareness. And recognition.

He pounces into my arms, his mouth locking onto mine. His lips and tongue are cool as they wrestle with mine, but they warm quickly along with the rest of him as one need gives way to another. Only when I begin to struggle does he remember that I, at least, still need to breathe. He smiles, unabashed, as he reluctantly breaks the kiss.

Miss me? he asks, breathless. His lips do not move, but his eyes speak, and somehow I hear him.

"Yes," I sigh, reaching up to pluck a bit of leaf from his hair, smoothing it back into place. "Oh, yes."

My hand lingers, tracing the contours of his ear, and we both laugh. I remember when I'd checked to see if they were pointed. He presses against me, and again, we kiss.

How long this time? He pulls impatiently at my shirt, ripping some of the buttons before finally tearing it away.

I shrug and shake my head, not wanting to release him either. He moans softly into my mouth as he runs his fingers through my chest hair, and I run mine around his sensitive nipples. "Ten," I murmur. "Ten long, pointless days and even longer nights."

His face clouds, and I regret my words.

"It doesn't matter." I smile gently into his dark, uncertain eyes then kiss his chest. "You're here now. That's all that matters."

It is what he needs to hear. His face lights up, and we begin again, touching and pulling as we fall to the floor. The clothes go quickly and are forgotten as skin presses against the skin.

The sound of rain is mixed with the bumping and shoving of furniture unfortunate enough to be in our way as we make love on the floor. We wrestle and roll, chest against chest, thighs grappling, hips grinding for maximal groinal advantage as hands and mouths caress and devour. We are full-body lovers, Michael and I, using everything given us to pleasure and be pleasured. In that, at least, neither of us have changed.

God, you feel good! Michael rises up above me, his eyes aglow as he pins my wrists to the floor. His fangs are quite visible now, sharp and shining with desire. He pushes himself up with his toes, his hips undulating in a way that rubs our urgent genitals together.

"So do you," I moan. His grip is supernaturally strong, and I can do nothing as his cock duels with mine, his hardness rubbing the length of mine between our writhing bodies as our scrotal sacks nestle and bounce, driving our heat ever higher.

He relents, and I am pinning him to the ground. I bend to lick the sweet smoothness of his chest, teasing his dark brown nipples with my teeth, and now he struggles in delightful agony beneath me.

The dance of flesh continues in ever-shifting turns, each flowing smoothly into the next, the lead being the desire of the moment, the where and how we wish to touch and be touched.

Yesss, Michael sighs in silent, close-eyed bliss as we lay hips to face, his hot hard cock pressing past my lips as mine presses past his. Our hands explore each other, touching and guiding as we settle into the familiar ease of the sixty-nine.

I close my eyes, enjoying the trembling in Michael's body as my tongue swirls about his glans, driving him to a near frenzy. It is my secret pleasure, the feeling of control, of mastery, that having his cock in my mouth brings. I concentrate on the moment and take my pleasure while it lasts, knowing he will not permit what I miss so much.

Michael responds in kind, teasing and licking me in return as his fingers seek out the secret places in my ass that he knows so well. He is hungry this night for more than blood. I fuck his mouth with mounting need as my balls pull up tight in their sack, excited to bursting by the danger-thrill feel of coaxing fangs along the urgent shaft.

Gripping his smooth hips, I take him deeper into my mouth, fanning the flames higher with my lips and tongue. Feeling other yearnings. Secretly hoping that maybe, this time, he'll give in

Please, Michael begs, his need echoed in fevered mouth and urgent hands. *Feed me...shoot it down my throat...I...I need it bad....*

The image triggers it. I cry out, muffled, pressing my hips forward as my cock swells and pumps within him, feeding him at last. The pleasure waves run through me like a hammer as pulse after pulse of hot white life is spurted and swallowed. It is love and life in the most intimate form, and I lose myself in the inexpressible timelessness of the moment.

That was...wonderful!

Michael is kissing me, and I realize that we are lying face to face again and that his cock left my mouth unspent. I kiss him back and smile, not intending to bring it up, but he senses my disappointment. He props himself up on an elbow, raising an eyebrow.

Okay, what's the matter?

I laugh. Even without his speaking, I hear the words with all the inflections I remember.

"Why won't you ever let me finish you? I miss it too, you know."

His face grows serious, and he runs his finger along my chest, tracing little patterns in the hair.

It's not the same thing. Your cum is like blood to me. But my cum is blood, and it could turn you into what I am. Are you ready for that?

I start to answer but hesitate, unable to say yes but unwilling to say no. "Maybe."

Well, I'm not.

Michael stands up and goes to the window, staring out into the darkness, and suddenly, the floor is a cold and lonely place to be. I rise slower and stand behind him.

You don't know what it's like, he insists, his reflected eyes avoiding mine. *Not knowing who you are, where you are. Not...* he shudders. *Not remembering the things you do half the time.*

"Sorry." I put my arms around him and hold him, and he leans back, folding his arms around mine. We do not speak for a long time. When I lead him away from the window, he does not resist.

Upstairs, we lay together in the brass bed—his bed, before—and listened to the rain. I put on some music, songs he remembers, and he rests quietly in my arms. He needs the familiar, and I try to give it to him.

Another song begins, and Michael wants to dance. It is our song, the first one we ever slow-danced to. We move to the center of the room and come together again in the moonlight, our naked skin warm between us. Laying our heads on each other's shoulders, we circle slowly in the night, playing that one song over and over again.

Finally, the music stops, and we do not start it again. We begin to explore each other anew with small kisses and caresses, our yearnings rising insistently between us. I slip my hand lower between his buttocks, looking into his eyes as I probe him gently in the opening gambit. He nods, then brings my hand up to his mouth, looking back into my eyes as he teases my fingers with his fangs. I smile, then kiss him deeply as we head back to the bed.

We prolong the anticipation with a bit of mutual voyeurism, Michael lying down on his belly, looking back over his shoulder at me as I oil up my cock. I gazed down at his lean, smooth body, his legs spread, and ass up in open invitation. Then, slowly, we begin.

Michael moans soundlessly as I enter him, arching his back against my chest, a shudder of pleasure/pain running through him. I lay myself across his back as I push in further, entwining my arms and legs with his, taking him, possessing him. It is what he wants. It is what I need.

My cock grows harder and thicker inside his incredible tightness, his sheath rippling the length of my shaft with each stroke. A side benefit of his change.

Having fun? Michael asks playfully, sensing my thoughts.

"Yeah." I shove deeper, and he gasps in silent, close-eyed pleasure. "You?"

Our love-making grows intense. Driven. Michael claws the sheets in ecstatic abandon as I buck and pump into him, his fangs nipping and teasing my fingers and hand. He has not drawn blood yet, but he will.

"Michael, I...."

so good...

"I'm...."

feels so good....

"I'm gonna...."

tastes so good....

"I'm gonna cum...."

inside me....

My balls contract in a warning. I cry out, ramming my cock in deep just as his fangs sink into my wrist, and suddenly I am filling him, feeding him from both ends, a double helping of everything. Waves of pleasure shudder back and forth between us, fading away at last and leaving us as one.

Afterward, we talk softly in the remaining night about little things, lover things, things from before. I have learned not to ask about other things, things he either does not know or will not tell. It does not matter. He is here.

Still, in the quiet moments between us when we speak through touch alone, I cannot help but wonder. Why did twenty years go by before he came back? How did he find me without memory to guide him? And above all, why me? I was not his first lover, though he was mine. Neither was I his last. And the time we were together was brief, however large a place it holds in my heart.

It does not matter. I do not care. I am the one he chose to return to. And now he is here. It is enough.

Dawn has come, and Michael has gone. The first light of morning falls softly on the empty place beside me in the bed, and I feel the pang of loss and longing once again. I did not see him leave. I never do. The morning comes, and he is gone.

I slowly sit up. There is no hurry to rise. The day has little to offer since Michael's return to my life. Only the night holds the promise of something better.

As I dress, one of the sketch pads catches my eye. The cover has been folded back and left open to a new page. I pick it up and turn it to catch the light.

It is Michael's gift, the thing worth a thousand words. He has drawn us together, asleep, my arm wrapped protectively around his chest, his hand clinging to mine. Strength and innocence. Trust and love. And, somehow, a promise of something eternal.

The Nine Parts of His Inhuman Soul

Eric LaRocca

Each part of him had been removed.

Cut out, scattered like unusable offal from slaughtered livestock.

The plants he had once cared for, wedding gifts, expensive souvenirs from European vacations—all unceremoniously discarded with the formality of weekly trash disposal. Whether they were displaced by time or hands eager to dismiss him, Julian was uncertain. Regardless, he was amazed to find, after only two years, the slightest indication of his presence had been cleaned from what was once his home.

He searched for remnants of himself in the only place left to look—the sweetness of his ex-lover's face. Like a lost child, he hunted for something familiar—the lines spider-webbing around Oliver's mouth from when he had made him laugh, the small divots in both cheeks from when Julian had made Oliver smile.

None of them seemed to linger.

Instead, he was met with Oliver's lips pulling downward and his vacant doll-like eyes—an expression so grim he resembled a father burying the corpse of a newborn.

"There's something I need to tell you," Oliver said as he stood on the porch of the small Dutch colonial. He pulled his collar around his neck, an autumn chill wrapping its fingers around him.

Julian could hear something pitched at the back of Oliver's throat, whistling like the wind of a distant thunderstorm.

Oliver pivoted from the entryway and ambled back into the kitchen. But Julian remained frozen at the threshold, unable to pass until a proper invitation had been granted.

Oliver turned, cursing himself for his forgetfulness.

"Come in," he said. "Please."

Julian sensed an invisible hand pull him across the threshold and into Oliver's home—the hand that probably commanded all monstrous creatures like him and gave permission to rise when it was safe to do so.

As they meandered through the house, Julian stole a moment to admire the man he once loved—still loved, in fact. The year in Julian's absence had not been kind to Oliver. Once generous shoulders now buckled like the framework of a loosened marionette doll, eyes offered a listless stare like the waxen look of an oil portrait. Oliver shuffled as if his moving parts were tenuously bound together like the limbs of a water strider.

Julian noticed himself slowing down, and his every movement was calculated more deliberately as if he were nearing something as delicate as a baby hummingbird. Noticing Oliver's eyes avoiding him at all costs, he watched as his ex circled the island at the center of the kitchen and resumed his work on the cutting board.

Finally, something familiar: a pile of pomegranates.

His favorite.

Some intact, freshly washed, and glistening wet. Others were split in half with blood-red honeycombed innards spilling across the countertop like marbles. Whether Oliver intended them as a peace offering or an insult remained unclear to Julian.

Surprising himself, Julian reached across and plucked one from the cutting board. He popped it in his mouth and pocketed the seed beneath his wilted tongue in an effort to revive a game they used to play.

The rules were simple: tuck a pomegranate seed in one's cheek and keep it there as long as possible without crushing it. Oliver looked at him, bewildered, as if he were enacting some childish ritual completely foreign to him.

"I wasn't sure if you'd come," Oliver said, brandishing a knife and carving one of the fruits in half. There was a noise hissing beneath his tone, a hurricane screaming itself raw to Julian—a voice saying, "I wish you hadn't."

"Did I have a choice?" Julian asked. It pained him to speak, the muscles in his throat as immovable as bedrock.

After all, it had been a year since he had used his voice. He had rehearsed different things he had planned to say to Oliver—speeches he had delivered to worms and maggots swarming in the small coffin he called home—but all opportunity seemed to slip away from him. He could hardly remember what he had wanted to say.

Of course, Julian didn't have a choice. Oliver had called to him like each year since his first resurrection. The marks on Oliver's throat resembled small coins reflecting in the sunlight and had barely healed since Julian's last visit. Julian sensed the crotch of his pants tightening at the thought of biting Oliver—ravaging him—once more. But he knew he wasn't allowed to drain him, or they would never let him return for his yearly reappearance.

"I—didn't think you'd come back after last—" His voice trailed off; the remainder of the sentence too cautious to tiptoe from his tongue.

Julian's eyes wandered to the empty dining room table, noticing an assortment of framed photographs facing away from him as if his presence would insult them. He imagined what the pictures might contain—photographs of Oliver and his new husband on a breeze-swept cliff overlooking the Mediterranean coast, the two pushing vanilla frosted cake into one another's mouth on their wedding day.

"Is he upset?" he asked.

"He's moving his mother into a nursing home in Haverhill tonight," Oliver said, wiping his fingers across his apron.

That didn't answer the question, though. Oliver's prowess at sidestepping uncomfortable subjects was something akin to a carpenter ant's instinct to skirt around a bead of water to avoid drowning.

"He knows I'm here?" Julian asked.

"He remembers the day," Oliver said. "Too well."

His words dangled in the air, thick and viscous. Julian followed Oliver's eyes to the calendar hung beside the refrigerator—six letters written inside the small box for Tuesday, October 31st: JULIAN. All capitals. The edges of each letter were thick and black—as if signaling the arrival of Armageddon.

"Do you have an arrangement when he has a visitor?"

Oliver tilted the damp cutting board, fat red seeds skating off the ledge and filling a glass bowl. He swallowed, his hands seeming as unsure as his brittle, thin voice. "He doesn't. Not once."

Julian leaned closer, testing Oliver's comfort the way a

child might approach a small animal. "You said his father was turned last year."

"He doesn't come," Oliver said, tipping the bowl beneath the faucet and rinsing the seeds.

"Must be a reason why." The way Julian said it even startled himself, mouth flicking out the words as if his tongue split down the middle the way it was supposed to.

"He doesn't want him to visit," he said. "Even if you are granted permission to return one night a year."

"I'll ask for him when I go back," Julian teased.

Oliver's eyes snapped to him, pupils filling with dread. "Don't."

The cruelty in his tone was enough to halt Julian from coming any closer. Fear had made its home across Oliver's face, and Julian's stomach turned at the fact he had placed it there with such ease. He relished in the breaks of conversation—fleeting moments when he could pretend he was no longer the unwelcome house guest.

He wondered if a gentleness remained hidden somewhere deep in some secret part of Oliver he had never revealed to him in the ten years of their marriage. As much as he wanted to search for a semblance of affection thawing from beneath his icy glare, he knew his time was limited.

"What did you have to tell me—?"

Oliver inhaled through his nostrils, head lowering until he resembled an Encaustic rendering of a saint in the act of supplication. The soundless question hung in the air for a moment before he finally pushed it out: "How many more times are you going to come back to me?"

The words crept from the corners of his lips, slick looking as if they were made of oil. Julian braced himself as best he could. He watched Oliver's eyes wander over him, picking apart his every weakness, from the rings of dirt caked beneath his fingernails to his arms flowering with flecks of blight. Wincing, he cowered as Oliver's eyes continued to perform an invisible autopsy on his rotted body—the craftsmanship of his embalmer's technique no match for Oliver's judgment.

Julian swallowed hard, clearing the gravel from the pit of his throat. "Until you tell me not to anymore. That's how it works."

"I told you last time," he said, his voice cracking apart like an eggshell.

"You said he didn't want me here," Julian reminded him. "You didn't tell me what you wanted. I keep coming back because you want me to."

Oliver looked as if he knew he was right—the guilt etched into his mouth as his lips creased.

"That's why I'm glad you came," he said. "There's something I need to tell you. I am—" Oliver stopped himself, searching his mind for a moment and finally settling on adequate words. "We're going to have a baby."

His words hammered into Julian, pinning him against the wall until he could no longer move. Julian sensed his juiceless organs sag inside him as if they were filling with cement. His shriveled lips curled inward like elastic bands and glorified a hideous grin over which his sorrow had no control.

"I'm—due in March," he finished, rubbing his stomach.

Julian could scarcely speak. He sensed his joints tightening once more, muscles cooling until he could no longer feel anything. A mortician's blade wouldn't do much now; Oliver had already ripped him from stem to sternum.

"You've known for a while," Julian said, the hurt residing in his voice barely restrained.

"He doesn't think—" Oliver stopped, correcting himself. "I—don't think you should come back next year."

Julian circled the pomegranate seed beneath his tongue,

pinching it there as if it were the last thing keeping his every extremity from snapping apart like sticks of kindling. Of course, he hadn't anticipated the same bewildered yet passionate welcome he had received two years ago when he had first returned for the day; however, he hardly expected Oliver's eager dismissal after merely two visits.

It was frustrating to see Oliver in yearly increments—their every secretive meeting a dizzying snapshot of a narrative that didn't quite make sense to him. Moreover, a narrative in which he no longer played a role. He had given him full blessing to seek out new relationships in order to cure some of his loneliness, but he now felt like a homing pigeon tirelessly searching for a stretch of land in an infinite sea.

Even worse, he'd prefer to be compared to a pigeon as opposed to the monster he knew he was. His chest without a heartbeat, his hardened veins as if filled with wax, his sharpened fangs, his fever-yellow skin—all were evidence of his vileness. There was nothing human about him now, and he knew it.

Of course, Julian had entertained the occasional obscene thought of turning Oliver—of draining him until his body was pale and bloodless. But even in his most ravenous state, he could hardly rationalize making his beloved suffer such a terrible fate. He loved Oliver far too much to turn him into a creature that's allowed admittance to the world only one night a year. Although Oliver most likely resented him for the love Julian had shared with the nocturnal creature that had turned him, Julian's mind seldom returned to the vampire that had first transformed him.

"We talked about having a baby," Julian said. His voice—a pitiful whisper. "You were... too scared."

"Still am. I don't—"

"Want it?"

Oliver dumped the bowl of pomegranate seeds in the trash, and discarded the last of Julian's hopes with them.

"I think you should go," he said.

Julian knew it was more than a mere thought—it was a plea. He blinked. Tears weren't possible, but pain certainly was. He wondered if Oliver noticed the agony flickering in his bloodshot eyes because he seemed too pale, as if already apologetic.

"Tell me it's what you want, and I will," Julian said. "Bury me in your thoughts. We come back only because you want us to."

Oliver hesitated, eyes searching him—this time evidently not for proof of his monstrosity but rather a semblance of familiarity. Wide-eyed, desperate to recognize any hint of humanity remaining within him.

"I can't," he murmured, shaking his head. Eyes shimmered wet. "I buried myself with you that day."

The sound of Oliver's beating heart filled Julian's ears, and for a moment, he envied him. Envy was soon replaced by pity as he watched Oliver shrink, an invisible pine box casketing him. Knowing full well he might recoil from his touch, Julian reached for Oliver—bloated fingers pressing against his open palm.

"Then I have to keep coming back," he said.

Oliver did not hesitate this time. Lassoing Julian with his arm, Oliver pulled him close and pushed his mouth against his. His tongue—sweet like grenadine. Julian didn't resist as Oliver's hands frisked him, fingers carelessly peeling some of the mold growing in thick greenish-blue clumps from his face.

As they sank further into what felt like a permanent embrace, Oliver steered them into the bedroom. Easing himself onto the bed, Julian relaxed as he felt Oliver's weight shift on top of him. He was only too glad to let Oliver take control—this is what he had wanted, after all.

However, Julian couldn't help but notice there was still a remaining part of Oliver that seemed to hesitate slightly—the reluctance in his eyes, the unsure way he touched Julian as if he were manhandling a complete stranger. But Julian was more than certain for him. He commanded Oliver to be still for a moment—to relinquish all doubts, all misgivings until his desires had made themselves known to him. Oliver swayed unsteadily, finally returning to his body from the trance Julian had conjured. Only now did Oliver seem more assured and less pensive.

Oliver devoured Julian's permanent ghoulish smirk, tongue coiling around his and passing a soundless language between them that only their lips seemed to know. Julian raked his head back against a small pile of pillows, his cock stiffening as Oliver pushed his tongue across his face and whimpered softly in his ear.

After tearing off his pants and underwear, Oliver straddled Julian and undid his pants as well until the fat purple head of his throbbing cock sprouted from between his zippers. Julian watched, fangs beginning to unfurl, as Oliver grabbed him and gently teased the puckered pink lips frowning where Oliver's legs met. Oliver eased himself down onto Julian's shaft until his cock was swallowed to the hilt. Julian sensed himself harden as he stirred inside his beloved, thrusting in and out while Oliver gleefully bounced there with eyes rolling to the back of his head as if on the brink of orgasm.

Oliver leaned down, heating Julian's ear with his breath and begging to be fucked harder—to be ravaged, to be defiled. Cupping Oliver's ass with both hands, Julian thrust himself again and again into Oliver's hairless cunt as he writhed on top of him in ecstasy.

If Julian could have climbed inside Oliver and built a small nest there, he would have. He would have gladly been swallowed whole by the hairless slit residing between Oliver's thighs. Oliver seemed to know this, smiling at Julian as they made love and seeming to beg him to take him—ravenous beasts like the last two of a dying species.

It was then that Julian's fangs found Oliver's skin and pressed down, the warmness of his lover's blood rising there like a secret wellspring—a dark tide as black as oil washing over their naked bodies until they were consecrated and born anew.

When they were finished with their lovemaking, Julian was surprised how any semblance of humiliation was absent from him. Instead, he reveled in the frankness of his naked body—even the obscener aspects of his decomposing anatomy.

Whether Oliver merely chose to ignore the waxy spots of mold blooming across his pelvis or the leathery parchment texture of his skin, Julian was uncertain. Regardless, he seemed to pay little mind to the matter while mooring himself against him as if guarding his body from suffering any further decay.

"Did you ever see what your soul looked like?" Oliver asked.

Lost in thought, Julian unwillingly returned to his body at the prospect of conversation. "What?"

"You know," Oliver hinted. "When it first happened. When they took your soul from you, did you see what it looked like?"

This wasn't the first time he had asked. Usually, it was the sort of thing requested during their infrequent yearly meetings when Julian was feeling particularly sentimental or thoughtless enough to momentarily let his guard down.

Of course, other nocturnal creatures who had returned had regaled the bewildered masses with mystical tales of the liminal spaces existing between life and death; however, each account varied depending on the individual. Skeptics might have had grounds to criticize the claims even further if the reports weren't filed from the actual gravesides of the temporarily risen deceased on Halloween night.

Although he always wanted to tell him, Julian was intent on making this moment as memorable as possible.

"There are nine parts to the soul," Julian explained. "They took all but one of them."

Oliver straightened, pulling some of the sheets over him as if still embarrassed of the scars beneath both of his pectorals from where the surgeons had corrected nature's mistake. "Which one?"

"My name," Julian whispered. "They let me keep my name. That's the last thing that they take when we perish."

"But your soul?" Oliver asked, as if insisting. "You've seen it?"

Julian nodded.

"Is it beautiful?"

"I'll tell you next time," Julian teased.

Oliver lifted himself up, kicking off some of the bed sheets as a livid color filled his cheeks. "I told you. There can't be next time."

Julian wondered if Oliver was pleased to see him so bewildered, his contentment snatched by the root and dragged screaming from where he had planted it deep inside him. He wouldn't allow him the satisfaction of an ambush and instead pretended he had expected his cruelty.

"Then tell me to leave. Tell me it's what you want."

He waited a moment as if preparing his for the answer. "It is."

Drawing air through the hole where his nose once was, Julian made a soundless promise to him with merely a look.

Oliver's face softened as if he understood.

Pushing the pomegranate seed to the corner of his mouth, Julian blanketed it with his tongue even though he knew full well their game had already finished.

A small crowd gathered at the cemetery's entrance when they arrived. Oliver eased on the brakes as costumed children holding their parents' hands dashed across the rain-soaked lane, toting large handmade banners. Leaning against the window, Julian squinted to read some of the signs. One read: *Welcome back, Grandma.* Another was written in exquisite cursive lettering: *We love you, Madeleine.* The small coterie—comprised of all ages—assembled beneath a canopy of umbrellas beside the wrought iron gates with cheery smiles as if they were welcoming loved ones at the airport baggage claim.

All heads swiveled toward him as Julian climbed out of the car, eyes lighting up as if he were royalty. Gasps of excitement filtered throughout the crowd, children tugging on their mothers' sleeves and pointing. Three years after the first vampire had made an appearance, the novelty had yet to dissipate for some.

Julian awkwardly shifted from his seat, inching further onto the sidewalk as Oliver followed a few paces behind as if he were a disinterested parent. As they approached the gate, interest among the gawkers began to weaken as they turned their attention to a new arrival: a young boy limping down the headstone-flanked gravel pathway.

His poorly preserved face—blackened like a charnel pit and eaten away by thick lichens of mold. His exposed arms and legs—thatched with more evidence of decay. A middle-aged man and woman with armfuls of toys and fresh packs of blood raced toward him, showering him with affection undeserving of such a monster.

Another one arrived—this time, returning to the cemetery like Julian. He watched as the elderly man—maggot-eaten skin as transparent as wax paper and eyes dimmed of all light—shuffled past him with his wife's hand tucked beneath his arm. They exchanged muted "goodbyes," pecking one another with kisses. What must have been a ritual for several years now ended in a matter of seconds as the old man breezed through the gates without a second glance back, as if knowing he would eventually return. A caretaker carrying a small shovel trailed him as he wandered through rows of headstones toward an open grave. A large truck idled nearby, prepared to unload a flood of wet cement onto the casket when the creature was properly interred.

There was something far more terminal in the way Julian looked at Oliver. An understanding of finality and how he would not be coming back. He accepted his look without comment. It was what he wanted, after all.

Julian knew he would go wanting for a modicum of affection when saying "goodbye." After all, he was well aware this wouldn't be the end.

Julian would return in another way.

In its infinite power, death for an otherwise immortal predator had granted him the gift of clairvoyance. He envisioned the child Oliver and his husband would bring into the world—soft and pink—a little boy. They would name him Julian.

He saw his mouth. There, hiding in the infant's toothless smile: a small pomegranate seed.

Black Sambuca

Jeff Mann

I.

I sense him before I see him. He radiates power the way a glacier exudes cold or a woodstove heat. There, that broad-shouldered silhouette, that gleam of pale hair and skin beneath a leafy canopy of vines, on the edge of Piazza Viminale. *Ristorante Strega*, says the sign. He's sitting back in the quiet shadow of a remote corner—as my kind tend to—watching happy humans as they feast al fresco on aromatic Roman food and wine in the warm summer night. When a shapely waitress bustles over to seat me, all I have to do is murmur his name and she escorts me to his table. A man well known in Rome, it appears.

He rises, smiling down at me, and shakes my hand. Though, like me, he appears to be in his mid-thirties, I know he's much, much older than I. He's several inches taller too, easily six and a half feet, and more mightily built. "*Buona sera*, Derek Maclaine," he says. His grip is strong, very strong. It makes me want to wince. Already he's reminding me of my position.

He is the lord here, and I the supplicant. Not only is he older and stronger, but this is his territory. I am a mere tourist.

My centuries in the American South have made my manners immaculate, despite the displeasure I'm feeling at being the less powerful in our exchange. I meet his blue-fire gaze, then drop my eyes. "I much appreciate this audience, Mr. Colonna," I say.

"Call me Marcus," he says, still gripping my hand, then turns to the hovering waitress and orders for us both. "My guest will have Romana Black, and I my usual." Off she goes to the bright lights of the bar, leaving a hint of jasmine in her wake.

"She wears that scent for me." Marcus turns to me, face shifting from an expression both stern and impassive into a barely perceptible smile and then back again. "Welcome to Rome, Derek Maclaine," he murmurs, giving my hand another painful squeeze before releasing me and taking his seat. "Sit," he says, and I do. The man was once a Roman senator. He's accustomed to swift obedience. And in order for me to get what I want, I suppose I too must obey him.

As handsome as he is, my obedience might be more pleasure than pain. "Thank you, Marcus," I say, studying the high forehead, sharp cheekbones, and shoulder-length ash-blond hair. His lips are red and full, his chin cleft, with the shadow of a goatee about his mouth. "It's mighty fine to be in your great city at last."

"Isn't she luscious?" Marcus says, voice smooth as rose petal yet embroidered with a growl. "Roma, yes. But our waitress too. *Bella, bella.* Her breasts and hips…. She is, as you Americans say, my type. Her name is Nigella. One night I will have her. But why rush?"

I smile. "I hadn't noticed, sir, but yes, she is beautiful." I can't recall when I last called another man other than my father "sir." Before I was changed, back in 1730? No, there was that

Russian lord in St. Petersburg…and that Greek in Santorini, and, of course, Sigurd, the massive Viking warrior who turned me.

"Ah, yes. You are a sodomite. Which will make your payment easier on us both, I suppose. I myself enjoy both the sexes, as lovers, slaves, and prey. What is your type, Derek Maclaine? And do you have a lover?"

"Yes, sir, I do. A human one, back in West Virginia. His name is Matt. He's my type. One of my types. Shorter than I, burly, hairy, with a bushy beard. A country boy. From the mountains, like me. What we in America call a butch bottom. We've been together for a decade."

"What is his age?" Marcus says. The waitress arrives, placing a slender glass of yellow liquid before Marcus, a similar glass filled with black liquid before me. "*Grazie*, Nigella," Marcus says, voice soft. She smiles and departs.

"Matt is forty-five, sir."

"He is your boy, yes?" A lock of yellow hair falls over Marcus' brow; he brushes it back, takes a sip, rests his elbow on the table, takes his stubbly chin in his hand and rubs it.

"Yes, sir, though not my slave. He's too—as we say in the mountains—too hard-headed and ornery for that." I want to say, *You are almost as beautiful as he,* but I suspect, powerful as Marcus is, he can read my thoughts and can already feel my desire and the way that submitting to him both shames and arouses me.

"And is he graying yet?" Marcus takes another sip. I can smell in his glass the heavy scents of sugar and lemon.

"Yes, sir. His temples are streaked with silver. His beard is as well, and the hair on his breast. He is so handsome, so ripe, a man in the fullness of his years, but…."

Marcus shakes his head. "Yes," he sighs. "*Trista.* I did that for centuries. Loved mortals. Now…not so often. Will you turn him?"

"No, sir. I don't think so. I don't know."

"Well, your other types?"

"Ah, Jesus lookalikes!" I laugh. "I like to ravish Christs. Slender boys with shaggy dark hair and beards. They make fine sacrifices. Occasionally, as understanding as Matt is of my feeding needs, they make him jealous. I do tend to dote on men such as they. Sometimes, when Matt's away on business, I kidnap one for my amusement and keep him for a few days."

"And have you had one of our Roman Christs yet?" His blue eyes flicker over me. Hunger is there in his glance, deep and fierce.

"No, sir, not yet. As you recall from our correspondence, this is my first visit to Rome. I only arrived last night, and I was told not to feed until...."

Marcus' foot nudges my boot beneath the table. "Very good. Yes. It is well that you obey. I can tell from the gray in your hair that you need to feed. Soon, I promise. Meanwhile, please sample your liqueur. That is black *liquore di sambuca*, which, according to the bottle, 'captures the spirit and allure of the Roman night,' a sweet, dark night such as this one in which we meet, Scotsman." Another faint smile flickers around his lips. With the ball of his thumb, he rubs the tip of his right incisor: quick flash, sharp, white, anticipatory. "And tell me if tall blond dominant Roman aristocrats meet your fancy."

Undead for centuries, yet I can still blush. No reason to lie. Old and experienced as he is, he could tell if I did. "Not normally, sir. I tend toward dark-haired men. But there are exceptions. You are indeed not what I expected of a Roman." I take a sip—more sugar, the odor of anise.

"Yes, most of us are much darker than I. During my human days, my friends teased me for my fairness. They said that a warrior from Germania had infiltrated my mother's bed. During my days with the army, my men called me

Aquila Aurea, the golden eagle. Many of them loved me. My lovers called me *Splendidus*. From what I can sense, you might agree with them." The faint smile goes broad only for a second before returning to that intense gaze, that impassive expression. "You will be my lover tonight, Derek? My boy? You will pay the price we agreed upon? In return I will share my city with you whenever you please."

My face is on fire. I can only drop my eyes, sip my liqueur, and nod. The sambuca is as rich, sweet, and thick as old blood, strong blood.

"Do you like it? The liqueur?"

"Yes, sir, I do. In future, when I drink it, I will certainly think of you. And you, sir? What is your type?" I lift my glass, stare into its blackness, then put it down. *Stop fiddling, Derek. Stop being such a bashful flirt.*

"Ah, in men? Many, many kinds. Men both sleek like me and rough like you. Both young men and mature men. Both humans and vampires. Tonight, I want a man who is wild and proud and in need of discipline. I want a man accustomed to being in control to submit to me, to feed my strength. Have you ever known a man like that?" Marcus chuckles. "One whose manhood might be tempered and refined by submission?"

"Yes, sir." It's all I can do not to stammer. "I love those men too. It's just that it's been so long since I myself—"

"Relax, boy. We shall have a fine night on the Palatine Hill, there among the ruins of the Caesars. I will care for you well. I will not harm you...much. And you will be the stronger for it. I must admit, you are surprisingly handsome and well-mannered for a mountain barbarian."

I look up and laugh. His blue eyes probe me. I can feel his thoughts rummaging through my head, turning over the mental stones of memory and motivation.

"Oh yes, a barbarian," says Marcus. "You Scotsman were certainly trouble. Hadrian had to build that long wall against Caledonia."

"Yes, sir. And you all never conquered us." As subdued as my customary pride must be this night, I can't help but remind him. "We Scots were about the only folks whose asses you couldn't whip."

Anger flashes in his eyes for a split-second. Then he nods, another smile flickering over his stony features. "Not worth the trouble. Those thistle-sharp mountains? Those scruffy clans in their dirty tartans? Though you do present yourself well tonight." He leans forward, his glance roaming over my black jeans, black T-shirt, black cowboy boots, and the thorny tattoos on my left forearm. "You are a fine specimen of a...redneck? That is the expression?"

"My boots give it away, I guess. And my ink?" I can't help but grin. I must indeed look like a well-dressed hillbilly compared to him. An observer would find us an odd combination. On top of the tattoos and the informal attire, my hair is long, pulled back in a ponytail, and my goatee's like a biker's, bushy enough to braid. I most likely resemble a Hell's Angel trying to look nice but not quite pulling it off. Marcus, on the other hand, is the picture of a wealthy, pampered European, with his white silk shirt, beige linen pants, expensive watch, golden neck chain, and designer leather dress shoes. Scottish Highlander in my human years, Appalachian for most of my vampire existence, I can't hide my rough edges even when I try. Especially from a gaze as steady and searching as his.

"And your beard betrays you, *paganus, rusticus*. You look like a Confederate general. You remind me of Enkidu. In need of taming, I think."

"Enkidu? In the Sumerian *Epic of Gilgamesh*, right?

The hairy wild man who came down from the mountains to be the comrade and lover of the great hero Gilgamesh."

"You are better educated than I expected. That is correct. Let me see your bare chest, please, my mountain redneck, my Appalachian Enkidu."

My cock hardens beneath the table. I'd forgotten how exciting it is to be told what to do by a man much stronger than I.

"Here?" I say, half-turning toward the tables of diners.

"I own Rome. I do what I please. Tonight you will do what I please. Just a glimpse."

Blushing, I pull my T-shirt up to my neck, baring my belly and chest.

Marcus takes a long, low breath, staring at my exposed torso. "Just as I imagined. Hairy as a savage. As an animal in need of a rider. Finish your drink, boy, and I will give you a tour of the Palatine. I will break you. I will make your chill skin sweat."

II.

The ruins are fluted gray in the moonlight. Under flat-topped cypresses, upon the crest of the Palatine Hill, we explore the remains of imperial palaces long abandoned, strong with the scent of pines and, this late at night, closed to tourists. Rubble now, once the homes of Augustus, Tiberius, Septimus Severus, Domitian. The fragments of columns, arcades, fountains, even a small stadium. Below us, modern Rome steams in the night, the lights of traffic pouring along its streets like phosphorescent lemmings.

"Did you know any of them? The Caesars?" I stroke a clump of oleander bloom. It is silent here, save for the distant noises of traffic and the cheeping of summer insects in the bushes and trees about us. Moonbeams slant over Marcus' white face as he moves closer to me.

"A few. Caligula raped me. He was assassinated long before I could take my revenge. I was turned in the reign of Claudius." Marcus looks down at the ruined rocks of the Forum, illuminated by searchlights for the benefit of tourists, and toward the monumental buildings atop the Capitoline Hill. "Take off your shirt."

I pull the garment over my head. Marcus takes it, laying it carefully on a jagged chunk of marble he first brushes off with the side of his hand. He turns to me now, resting his hands on my shoulders. "So you have come to Rome to pay your respects?"

I gaze up at him, trying not to tremble. "Yes, sir."

"To the Caesars or to me?"

"Both." It is hard to meet his gaze, yet impossible to look away. My victims must feel the same when I entrance them. "In all my centuries, I have never come to Rome. It is more beautiful than I ever imagined. I would like your permission to linger here, and to return when I please."

"And you are ready to pay the price? For a nest in my realm? For the freedom to feed here? This is, I sense, a price you are unaccustomed to."

"I am unaccustomed, but I am ready," I say. "Sir."

Marcus nods. Moonlight gleams off his teeth, a true smile, wide with triumph. His fingers find my chest, stroking the thick fur there. I wrap my arms around his waist, bow my head, and lean against him. He tugs at my nipples, then the rims of hair around them, then the tangled bush of my beard.

"Strip," murmurs Marcus. He gives me a gentle shove backward. "And unbind your hair."

Boots first, then jeans, then the leather cord in my ponytail, discarded one by one in dry grass. Entirely naked, vulnerable, I stand before him, in warm Roman breezes, in the scent of wildflowers, in moonlight. I stare down at my exposed body, at my inked and muscled arms, at my hairy belly and chest, my hairy legs, trying to see myself as he sees me. It has been many, many years since I have submitted to another vampire, or felt undead lust raking me with such sharp zeal. Marcus' eyes are gleaming, the blue gone a fiery red.

"Shaggy brute," he whispers, tousling the long hair framing my face, ruffling my belly fur, patting the face of the Horned God inked into my left arm, the barbed wire band inked into my right. "Tattooed like your feral ancestors, those mad Celts. The antlered god of the Gauls, I see. God of beasts and mountains, yes? A hirsute, hard-cocked Dionysus. Apropos. My deity is Mithras. You will show him homage later."

From his back pocket, Marcus fetches something gleaming. "A surprise," he says, holding it before me. I can feel it already, the shining power that can make my head swim and my muscles grow feeble. Silver. He's brandishing a pair of leather-lined silver handcuffs. Open and ready to use.

I step back, unsure. "Sir? You never mentioned this. I never agreed—"

Marcus outflanks me in a split-second, faster than I can further react. Again the difference in our powers gives me some sense of how outmatched my human victims must feel. He pulls my wrists behind me before I know he's there. But rather than subdue me further, rather than locking the cuffs, he simply stops. I stand there, trembling. A blunt hardness that must be his erection bumps my back. It seems that subduing me is exciting him as much as being subdued is exciting me.

"Trust me, barbarian. I will make this sweet. I will make you enjoy this." Marcus sniffs me and noisily licks his lips. "Ah, you are sweating now. You stink. You smell like mud and grass and woodland. You smell like the Gallic prisoners I used to take in Mamertine Prison, only yards from here. Your hair"—he takes a strand in his teeth and pulls—"and your unruly beard remind me of them." He nips the skin over my spine. I can feel his chin's scratchy stubble. "Dirty and wild...forest scum, so proud at first before they were chained and raped and broken. Warriors become slaves... they sobbed and shook beneath me. They lay in the prison's straw and dung and wrapped their mighty arms about my feet and begged me for release. Will you sob for me?"

"No," I say, teeth gritted. "I'm no slave."

"But you will submit?"

"Yes."

"You might sob yet. We shall see." The cuff snaps over my right wrist, painfully tight. The leather saves me from that terrible burn, but the poisonous silver's near enough to cause my knees to buckle. I would drop to the ground, but Marcus wraps an arm around my neck and heaves me upright. His knuckles graze my ass-cheeks before the cuffs lock just as tightly about my other wrist. He releases me; groaning despite myself, hands firmly secured behind me, I sink to my knees and fall onto my side in the grass. The silver weakness shudders through me, nauseating.

Marcus nudges my chin with his elegant shoe. Then he steps back, toes off each shoe, and strips, very slowly, laying each article of clothing in the grass with such care you'd think the fabric were fragile as glass. I roll with discomfort onto my cuffed hands to watch as his muscular body, as hard and perfectly defined as a gymnast's, is revealed. Entirely naked, he stands over me, astride my waist. His body is pale, smooth, gleaming like the face of the moon, a study in Carrara marble, with a dusting of gold. "I was quite the athlete when I died," he says, running hands over his curved pectorals, big brown nipples, and ridged stomach before taking his fur-clouded cock in hand. It lengthens rapidly in his grasp, escaping its skin-sheath. It is intimidatingly huge. The head glistens, slick and knobby, moonlit pommel of a sword. I am, I suspect, soon going to be hurting bad.

By now I'm hard as well. "I can see your appreciation, boy." Laughing, Marcus presses a bare foot against my cock. "Stiff with shame, I see. I know men like you. I know them and I love them. There is a secret slave, very frightened yet very hungry, inside that coarse Scots warrior, is there not? Something tender, submissive, shy? A boy eager to suffer, to endure, to be enveloped and devoured and rocked like a child?"

I shake my head, but my denial has no power. There's my body's unarguably honest answer, beneath Marcus' foot, hard between my thighs. He presses down, and I gasp.

"Not much fight in you with those cuffs, Highlander?" He presses harder.

"No, sir. Silver saps my strength almost entirely. How did you—?"

"Handle silver without consequence? After my first thousand years it lost its power over me. Now it barely makes me tingle." He lifts his foot from my crotch only to press his sole against my mouth. "Lick, boy. Let Caledonia at last give Rome her due."

I run my tongue over his foot. Hard as embossed steel. Smooth and taut as the skin of ripe fruit. He nudges me onto my side. I moan as he pushes his big toe into my mouth.

"Suck, barbarian."

I do. I suck, lick, nibble. More toes join the first, my mouth crammed full. He tastes like metal and wind. I stretch my jaw, taking him further in.

Abruptly he pulls his foot from my face and steps back.

"Get up here, wild one, my Enkidu. It's time to show your fealty."

With effort I rise to my knees, and, kneeling, shuffle over to him. I've hardly opened my mouth before his bulky cock's thrust inside me to the hilt, balls pressed into my beard. His hands grip my long hair, holding my head still while he rides my face. My throat expands, contracts. I choke and slobber. My gorge rises; I force it back. He pounds my mouth steadily, his pre-cum streaking my tongue with salt. Drool drips off my chin. I try to bring subtle techniques into play, try to lick the head, run my tongue up and down the shaft, but to no avail. Marcus wants nothing but a hole, a deep one. He batters the back of my throat the way Hebridean oceans batter sea cliffs, unceasing, inexhaustible.

Just when I think the savage throat-beating I'm getting will soon insure me a white mouthful of sex-foam, Marcus lifts me by the arms, spins me, and throws me onto my belly in the grass. He's on top of me a split-second after I hit the ground, one hand on the back of my neck, shoving my face against the earth, an arm wrapped around my chest. "Ah, yes. This is what you came to Rome for, is it not?" he whispers in my ear, his cock bumping my buttocks. "I enter you; you enter my kingdom? Yes? Yes?"

"Yes," I groan. Heat-dead grasses scrape my face; Roman earth dusts my lips. I grit my teeth, readying myself for the pain.

But Marcus is taking his time. His lips brush my ear. "How long, barbarian? How long since you were taken this way?" Beneath me, his fingers trap a nipple. His nails begin to dig.

"Sir, my lover Matt sometimes…we switch. We even… we have silver cuffs at home."

"Ah, so you bottom occasionally? Then this will not be as grand a trauma as I'd imagined? A pity. How long since another vampire took you then?"

"Half a century, sir. In Santorini."

"Yes? The blood is strong there. Older even than mine." Marcus' hand leaves my neck, positioning his cock against my tightness. "You want this, do you not?"

Again, I know better than to lie. "Yes, sir. I don't want to want it, but I do."

"Beg me, my hirsute captive," Marcus sighs. "Beg me to take you."

I hesitate only for a second. That long submerged part of me is rising, eager. "Please, sir. Please, Marcus. Take me...." I arch my ass, rub it against him, brush his hard belly with my bound hands. "I can't fight you, I'm too weak. I'm your captive, sir. Do what you please."

"And so I shall." He slips down my body. His fingers play over my ass, tugging on the cheek- and cleft-hair, and then his hands clutch my hips and his teeth sink into my right buttock.

"Huhhhh," I gasp into the grass. His lips clamp down, sealing the sudden wound, sucking hard. I can feel my strength receding further, the silver-weakness mingling now with blood-loss.

The suction stops. Liquid smeared between my ass-cheeks. Lubrication of my own blood. I grunt as his finger enters me. I buck back onto his hand. Another finger slides inside. "Open. Open for Rome," Marcus whispers. His muscled weight, like a great sculpture, settles atop me, his cockhead pressing against me, his arm wrapped around my torso.

"Be easy, Highlander. I will care for you well."

I nod, trying to will myself open. His cockhead replaces his fingers, easing inside. Damn, so thick. Pain spasms through me, forcing out a whimper.

"Easy, boy." To my surprise, Marcus does not simply shove it in and rape me, as the earlier mouth-pounding suggested that he might. Instead, to my relief, he moves the head in and out in short strokes. He pulls out, adds more bloody lube, and pushes the head in again. More shallow strokes, till the pain at last recedes and he can sense my readiness. Then, very slowly, with surprising gentleness, he slides entirely inside, filling me completely. More waves of pain; I give a loud, deep moan. Marcus' hand grips my jaw, palm pressed tightly over my mouth.

"Quiet now, boy. There, there. Yes." Cocking his hips, he moves slowly in and out, in and out. I moan inside his muffling grip. "Ruffian. Lovely, smelly, hairy Scot. I will use you now, mountain man, will I not? Beg me to use you. Do you not want used? Used hard?"

He pulls out, resting his cockhead against my entrance. The sudden emptiness is an ache.

"Use me, sir. Hard, please, sir. I can take it." Muttering into his palm, I flex my ass-cheeks, grinding back against him.

"So reluctant to be ridden, now so eager to be used? If you insist." Marcus thrusts, quick and hard, shoving his entire length up inside me. I wince, gasping against the tight gag of his hand. A steady pounding begins. Cuffed, silver-weak, I lie there entirely helpless, impaled by bliss, deep grunts—"Huhh, huhhhh, huhhhh, huhh!"—forced out of me by the rhythmic hammering of his hips. Marcus's growl is as steady as my grunts are staccato.

He's off me before I know it. Again I'm aching and empty. Not for long, I sense. Seizing my bushy goatee, Marcus drags me across the grass to a broken column lying on the ground. He heaves me across it, bends me over. My face and knees are sunk in dead grass, my ass cocked in the air. He fang-nips both cheeks, spreads them, roughly cock-shoves up inside me and begins pummeling me anew.

I've no sooner started a new series of rapturous, stuffed-full-to-the-brim grunts than his right hand's again clamped over my mouth. His left hand finds my left pec. He manhandles the thick flesh, tugs painfully at the chest pelt. "A better angle, is it not?" Marcus pants into my tangled hair. "And a small price for all of Rome?"

What ecstasy it is to be completely vulnerable and completely owned, thoroughly plowed. I had almost forgotten. Nodding, I close my eyes, spread my thighs, push back onto him, and grip him from inside, as if I were squeezing the handle of a sword. "Ah, yes. Very nice. You are skilled for a dirty savage," Marcus says, increasing the speed of his thrusts. "You have learned well beneath my predecessors."

Smiling beneath his palm, I squeeze and relax, squeeze and relax. He rides for a bit, sighing with delight, letting the sweat build up between us, before he says, "I will hurt you now, boy. Yes?" Marcus pants into my ear. "You are ready to suffer for me? I may mark you?"

I grunt an affirmation, nodding against his firm grip. Immediately his fingernails sink deep into my nipple. I clench my teeth as he brings blood, twists and tugs the tiny nub of flesh, cuts deeper still.

Keeping one hand over my mouth, with the other he rakes my torso, my nipples, and my back with his sharp fingernails, leaving long, deep wounds. Blood wells up, trickling into my chest hair, down my spine. "And now, I think...." He shifts the position of his loins just a fraction, pulls back, shoves forward hard. My eyes roll, my fangs gnash my tongue, my own blood tinges my mouth.

"Here, I think, is the bodily seat of your submission, yes? This spot here?" Marcus chuckles. "Am I right, forest trash? Wild one so sweetly tamed?"

Yes, deep inside me he has found what few men have ever found, the point that makes me shake with such great pleasure. I go wild, bucking and writhing in his arms, crying out against his hand, trying to pull him into me even deeper. Giving my chest one last savage clawing, he locks his arm around my head and sinks his teeth into my neck.

The sucking begins—an irresistible gravity, a riptide more and more intense—hard and steady to match the pounding below. Within a minute, I'm immobile, sprawled limply across the column that once bore the weight of empire, rocking helplessly inside his thrusts. I hear him hissing against my split skin, feel him stiffening atop me, pumping my depths. Then Marcus's bloody hands grip my shoulders, his fangs slip from my flesh. He gives a shout, a final thrust, gushes semen into me, and collapses.

Blood tickles my neck. The column's marble is cold against my belly; my master's weight is great upon my back; my hole's a throbbing circlet of fire. The grass before my eyes smears, a brittle gold. That grades to red, then unbroken black.

I wake cradled in his lap. He is rocking me, blond hair curtaining his face. Again that faint smile. Tenderly he caresses the blood-ooze claw-trails his nails cut into my chest. I try to embrace him, only to find myself still weak, still cuffed. His lips meet mine. I can smell and taste my own blood in his kiss.

"You will be scarred for a time," Marcus says. "My nails leave welts even undead bodies have difficulty healing." He runs a finger along my chest, daubs up some blood, and laps it off. "But you are even more beautiful scarred, no? And these scars will mark you as mine during your stay in Rome."

From the seat of a ruined altar, he rises, lifting me into his arms. "The temple of Cybele once," he says, wistfully. "You should have seen it as it was." Enervated, I lean against him, wrists throbbing in the tight cuffs. Birds are singing somewhere. "Almost dawn, yes," he says, carrying me through aromas of pine, crunching of needles, then beneath an arch and down a long underground tunnel. "You may use this nest in future, if you please," Marcus says. He shifts me with ease from his arms to his shoulder, then edges aside a flat rock. Here, a grave large enough for the both of us. He lowers me gently onto my side, climbs in after me, and pulls the rock in over us. "I have hidden our clothes nearby. We will spend the day together here, my bound barbarian," Marcus says, gripping my cuffed hands and pulling me against him. We kiss, lengthily and deeply, before he presses his hairless chest against my mouth and says, "I can feel your famine. Drink, boy."

"Thank you, sir," I whisper. "Gladly." My tongue finds his nipple. I tease it into hardness, then push my fangs into him. He sighs, running his fingers through my hair and along the gashes on my back. His semen oozes from my ass and trickles down my inner thigh. Dawn must be near, for sudden drowsiness washes over me. I fall asleep suckling Marcus's breast, feeling the old blood glow and shimmer inside.

III.

"We should have killed them all," Marcus grumbles. "What trouble those beasts have caused."

We are strolling through what remains of the Colosseum. He's dressed in a dove-gray suit, crimson tie, and leather loafers, I in camo pants, black work boots, and a black tank top that allows Marcus to savor the sight of both my tattoos and my fresh scars. At his request, my hair's unbound. It's approaching midnight of our second night together. The great broken bowl of the stadium is empty of tourists. We walk along the corridors, under the barrel vaults, and take seats where emperors once did. Only a few feral cats are our companions tonight, and the moon, nearly full. Before us is the cross erected by a long dead pope to commemorate the Christians who died here.

"Are they as troublesome in your land, my Highlander? The Christians?"

"Oh, fuck yes!" I snarl. "They're a plague. They run through my mountains like a virus. They befoul the air!"

Marcus wraps an arm around me. "You are passionate about this, I see."

I flush and nod. "I do hate them. The hard-core kind, at least. They've caused me and mine much grief. Still, forgive the language, sir. We 'forest trash,' as I believe you called me during that fine pounding.... I'm still a little sore, by the way. Not that I'm complaining." I rub my butt and grin. "We forest trash do tend to be dirty-mouthed. I don't mean to be vulgar. I suspect a sophisticated man like you is used to fairer-spoken friends."

Marcus pulls me against him. I lean my head against his chest. It is a great relief, to relinquish strength and control for a change. "But you *are* vulgar. And I love it. I grow weary of refinement sometimes. Yes, we should have fattened our lions more efficiently. And speaking of flashing fangs and vigorous devouring, are you ready for your gift? You took little blood from me before you slept; your hair and goatee are still silvery. It's time to remedy that."

"Yes, I'm ready. What have you been up to?" Marcus has shown me several sights tonight—the Forum, the Capitoline, the Arch of Constantine—but before that tour, he'd left me silver-cuffed for several hours in our Palatine tomb while he "attended to business."

"Come with me." Marcus rises and takes my hand. "It's five minutes from here, down Via San Giovanni de Laterano."

Leaving the ancient stadium, we make our way past well-lit cafés, noisy, fragrant restaurants. We hold hands, the sleek aristocrat and the undead mountain man. God help the homophobic human who might object. But we meet with no objections, just a few stares, and soon we are swathed in shadow again, slipping down a narrow street and then inside the colonnaded courtyard of a church.

"San Clemente," Marcus says, pulling open the broad wooden door and ushering me inside. "I worship here."

"A Christian church?"

"No, no. Come, come." Marcus takes my hand. He's moving fast through the dimness, leading me past columns, mosaics, and choir screens—Christian irrelevancies—then through a swinging door and down broad stone steps. Here is a lower floor. I can make out bare stone walls, a distant flicker of candlelight; I can smell earth and human sweat, hear a faint, very human moaning. "Here?" I say. My fangs throb and lengthen.

"Not yet, young one, eager one. First you must pay homage."

Down another flight of steps, a deeper level yet. The sound of rushing water.

"Beneath the floor. The Cloaca Maxima, ancient Rome's sewer. That is what you hear." Marcus pulls me down a corridor to a doorway in the rough wall. "Here, here is where we need to be. The Mythraeum." Behind a locked grate is a low-ceilinged cave, a white marble altar flanked by stone benches. Marcus fetches a key from his pocket; the padlock snaps open; we enter the shrine.

"The Lord Mithras. He is the god of soldiers." Marcus runs his hands along the low reliefs. "Here, see, he sacrifices the bull. He cuts its great throat. And here, here are the dog and serpent. They drink the blood." He grips my shoulder. "On your knees, *rusticus.*"

I do as I'm told, kneeling beside him. Closing his eyes, Marcus mouths a few words I can't make out. Bowing my head, I give thanks to this foreign warrior god—for the splendid man by my side, for his beauty, ruthlessness, and strength, for his marble-white, marble-hard muscles, for his sharp golden desire.

Marcus tugs my beard. I jerk with surprise, then rise. His arms enwrap me, hugging me hard. "The god gives his approval. Now for your gift."

Back along the corridor and up one flight of steps. "This was a fourth-century church," says Marcus. "It also makes a fine feast-hall for my coven." There's a distant sound of sobbing. We follow it, turning several corners before coming into the low nave. I stare down the rows of double columns and flickering candelabra, to the stone canopy of the baldacchino at the far end, the high rectangular altar beneath it, and, most especially, what lies atop that altar. I growl deep in my throat. I run my tongue over my fangs.

"You are pleased? You said you doted on Christs."

"Oh, fuck. Oh, yes!" My lip curls up; I snuffle the rich air, heavy with terror and sweat.

Bound belly-down upon the altar is a young man. He's naked. His limbs are spread, wrists and ankles shackled and chained to the posts of the canopy. He stares at us with black, long-lashed eyes before breaking into soft fear-sobs again.

I cross the yards between us in a heartbeat. I wrap my fingers in his long black hair and pull his head back. Thick chain has been threaded between his teeth twice and padlocked behind his head, filling his mouth, muffling his cries. I study his handsome face, his tear-stained, half-crazed eyes. His weeping grows more violent still. He squints against his tears, then, unable to hold my gaze, clenches his eyes shut.

"His name is Francesco," Marcus says, somewhere behind me. "He's twenty-one. He speaks English fairly well. He lives with his old mother in the ghetto south of Rome; he uses his good looks to hustle tourists on the Spanish Steps. No one will miss him save her. He is yours now. To drain, enslave, keep, or kill."

The mention of murder evokes in Francesco a fresh bout of sobs, a few weak pleas his gag makes unintelligible. His white teeth grit the chain. He thrashes in his bonds. The steel links rattle and clink.

"*Aiuto. Per favore.* He's crying for help. So delicious." Marcus stands beside me now, fingering the spit-shiny chain between our prisoner's plump lips. "The boy's half-starved. But he gave us a fierce fight, like a wild animal. Rather than damage him badly, we drugged him. He's been kept bound down here for hours, watched over by some helpful minions of mine. He has little strength left. So he will do?"

"Ohhhh, yes," I hiss. "He's fucking *fine*. Thank you, Marcus!"

Francesco's face is thin, with prominent cheekbones and an aquiline nose. His shoulder-length hair is ink-black, as is his neatly trimmed goatee. He's very lean, rib-staves and hipbones ridging dirty skin. He's shiny with sweat; he smells of the street, of urine and long hot days without a bath. Other than the whiteness of his buttocks, his skin's an olive hue. Here and there are bruises, the result, I'm guessing, of the struggles he put up during his capture. I circle him now, stroking his long, thickly hairy legs, the muscles' straining definition. I caress the wet hair-nests of his armpits, the hair dusting his belly and chest. When I touch his buttocks, hard curves covered with fine black fur, he starts and shudders, shakes his head violently, cries out more chain-hampered words I can't make out. His fear's a liqueur, black and sweet. I laugh low, running a fingertip along his ass-crack. So moist, so warm, so aromatic.

"Oh, yes, he can guess what's coming next. Do what you please, barbarian. Use him as I used you." Marcus fetches two glasses and a bottle from the floor. Black sambuca again. He pours out the liqueur, hands me a glass, and clicks his glass against mine. I take a sip, lick the sugary anise off my lips, rest the glass on the corner of the altar, and strip.

I am naked now. Marcus brushes his fingers across my chest, along my arm. "White scars amid such black, black fur. Black tattoos against such white, white skin. Snow and coal. Comets streaking the darkness. The white wake of waves across the Mediterranean at midnight...." He sounds almost reverent, his eyes gone vague. "Ah, I am a bad poet. My apologies. But I am very glad you came to Rome, Derek Maclaine." He steps back, face again an ivory mask. "I may watch, may I not?"

"Yes, sir. I'd relish that." I leap up beside Francesco and stretch out. His face is pressed against the altar. I cup his bearded chin in my hand, turning his face toward me.

"Oh, you are so *fucking* beautiful," I sigh. "I am going to take you now, little Jesus. I am going to fuck you up the ass. Do you understand?" I smile, showing my fangs.

Francesco gives a sharp gasp. Francesco stares. Francesco pants with panic around his mouthful of chain. Drool wells through the links, dribbling onto my hand.

"I'm guessing you've been ass-fucked before? What with those eager clients on the Spanish Steps all salivating for your sweet favors?"

My prisoner continues to stare and pant, speechless. Customary behavior at the first sight of fangs.

"You'll answer me if you know what's good for you. I like my slaves mannerly."

"Uh huh," Francesco grunts, nodding.

"If you obey, you'll survive. If you struggle, you'll die. And if you give me enough pleasure, I might decide to own you, to keep you around. You understand? I need a slave here in

Rome, to watch over me and my new home. If I own you, I will care for you. And your worries will be over. You will live long and prosper."

Francesco nods. More warm drool, clear as water, drips onto my hand.

Fetching my glass, I slip down to kneel between my captive's widespread thighs. Across the pale curves and fuzzy crevice of his ass, I drip sambuca. I can hear Marcus' chuckle as I spread Francesco's cheeks and begin a deep nuzzling.

IV.

Francesco limps beside me through the old neighborhood of Vecchia Roma, over bumpy cobblestones, past pink and cream stucco walls. His stride's stiff, a little less than graceful. With good reason. Last night, after entering him as gently as Marcus entered me, I rode Francesco long and hard, on and off, for hours, wanting our first time to last. As I pounded him, I drank his delicious blood till he fainted. I sipped sambuca with Marcus till my captive came to. I beat his brown back and white buttocks with my belt, leaving bruises and welts, before climbing upon him, embracing him, entering him, drinking from him again. Francesco pleasured me with his ass, with his street-taught skills, coaxing cum from me time after time. He obeyed me in everything, didn't struggle or shout, was entirely acquiescent, limp with blood loss as dawn approached. We unchained him then, carried him to a secret crypt near the Mythraeum. We bound his hands and feet with rope. We tenderly gagged him with Marcus' silk tie. Marcus stripped, and the three of us lay together. Francesco spent the day between us, paralyzed and entranced, curled against the naked dead.

Tonight he is clearly hurting. But a slave is the last to complain. By now he bears a chain I have locked around his neck. By now he bears the marks of my teeth, on his buttocks, on his shoulders and neck. By now he is entirely my thrall.

This is the address. As Marcus promised, the medieval tower is in fine shape. I unlock the door, tugging Francesco after me by his collar. Together we ascend the winding stairs. At the top is a thick wooden door, and, behind that, the snug apartment. It is furnished beautifully, a mix of both antique and modern furnishings. And its little kitchen table is heaped with steaming food.

"Oh, *Signore!*" Francesco's belly growls. "May I?"

"Wine first, slave." I nod to the sideboard. Beside a bowl of red roses, Marcus has left a bottle of red wine, another of black sambuca, and several glasses. Francesco jumps to it, opening the wine and pouring out a glass. He looks up expectantly.

"Take off your clothes."

Francesco hurriedly shucks off his dirty garments. Again the arch of an expectant black eyebrow.

"Yes," I say, running a finger down the line of hair bisecting his flat belly. "You may eat. From a plate on the floor."

Not a second's hesitation. In a flash my handsome little Jesus has fetched a plate from the cupboard and is holding it out. He's positively salivating, staring first at me, then at the heaped table. I study his nakedness for a moment, his olive skin, his midnight-black pubic bush, his limp, uncut cock. This one will prove precious, I can already tell. And sweet Matt, back home, is going to love him. Matt's going to have the boy's legs in the air so damn fast. I can't wait to show Matt around Rome.

"How long since you last ate?" I sip the wine. It's very fine: cobwebs and blackberries. Of course. Aristocrats like Marcus always have superb taste.

"Three days, *Signore*." His mouth quivers.

"Poor boy. Let me." With utensils on the sideboard, I dole it out: *bucatini all'Amatriciana*, eggplant Parmigiana, roast pork with potatoes, spaghetti carbonara, Caprese salad, focaccia. I place the full plate on the floor, pull out a chair and take a seat. Francesco drops onto his elbows and knees, crawls over, and begins gobbling. I prop a booted foot upon his back and sip my wine, taking joy in his joy. When he's finished his first plate, I pile him up another. He hunches over it, shaggy black hair falling over his face, slurping and chewing with abandon.

Patting his prettily propped black-fuzzed ass, I leave him there to fill his belly while I indulge in a little exploration. Here are the big bed, the guest room, the study, and the secret panel where Marcus said it would be, behind which I will spend the days. And here, in the entrance hall, is an envelope I'd missed before, one addressed to me. I tear it open and read the note.

> *Enkidu, my handsome one, my wild forest trash,*
> *my musky butch bottom. Here is your new home.*
> *I hope it meets your needs. The rent is steep: your*
> *blood, your body, and your submission, whenever*
> *you are in Rome. I do not think you will mind*
> *paying such a fee. I hope your little Jesus enjoys*
> *his feast. Savor your sambuca. You said it would*
> *cause you to think of me. I hope that is so. I am*
> *leaving Roma for a week, for business meetings in*
> *Berlin. Meet me at the Pantheon two weeks from*
> *tonight. There is a vampire bar near there that*
> *serves an excellent blood orange gelato. Mithras*
> *bless you. Marcus.*

"*Signore*? I am done." It's Francesco, crawling down the hall on his hands and knees. His goatee and red lips gleam with grease. I lift him to his feet, kiss him, lick the oil from his mouth, and lead him into the kitchen. "Fetch me a glass of sambuca," I say, and he does. "Follow me," I say, hooking a finger under his chain collar and leading him out onto the balcony. I sit back in a lounge chair; my thrall sits cross-legged at my feet.

"Tomorrow we will move your mother into better housing. You'd like that?"

"Oh, *Signore*...." Francesco's eyes glitter wetly. He puts his face in his hands, then scoots over, wraps his arms around my legs, and rests his head in my lap. "*Grazie, grazie.*"

I take a sip of sambuca, looking out over the lights of Rome, the far, lit façade of Castel Sant'Angelo, the dome of Sant' Andrea della Valle. I stroke my slave's black hair. "Ain't you something fine? Hungry little savior. Furry little street-whore." I pull him up onto my lap, then push my thumb between his teeth. He licks it, then closes his mouth around it and gently begins to suck. I rock him as Marcus rocked me on the Palatine.

"Tomorrow, while I sleep, you'll take money and stock the shelves with all your favorite foods and wines. Buy yourself some handsome clothes as well. And some *limoncello* for when Marcus visits. He's fond of it, I think."

"*Sì, Signore*," Francesco murmurs around my thumb. His mouth is tight, wet, and hot.

"This is the reward of submission," I say, taking another sip of liqueur. "For both you and me." The moon's glow edges the eastern horizon. It will be full tonight, soon to shower the old quarter with pearl-white light. "When I'm done with this glass, I'm taking you inside. I'm going to knot a rag between your teeth and tie you belly down to that big bed and prop your hairy ass on pillows and fuck you till you bleed and come inside you and lap the blood from your luscious, hair-fringed hole and drink from your neck till you pass out. I'm going to keep you bound and rag-gagged till dawn; I'm going to hold you close all night. How does that sound, slave?"

Francesco nods, sucking harder, with all the intensity of the newborn. He suckles me and I rock him. Soon, just as it did in the time of the Caesars, in the time of the half-mad mercenary Renaissance popes and the fully mad Mussolini, the moon will rise, over the Colosseum, the Palatine, the Forum, over this renovated tower, older even than I. Bathed in summer moonlight, I will think of the few men I've loved. Angus McCormick, my first and thoroughly inescapable passion, who was stabbed to death, murdered by hateful Christians, on the Isle of Mull in 1730, the night I was turned. Sigurd Magnusson, the massive Viking vampire who gave me dark immortality. Mark Carden, my bushy-bearded Rebel soldier, who was shot through the head in the Battle of Chickamauga in 1863. Gerard McGraw, who bled to death in the trenches of Belgium in 1945. Matt Taylor, this century's spouse, who has many blessed years left, who waits for me in the mountains of home.

And now, I think, Marcus Colonna, who flies tonight to Berlin. Other than Sigurd, my maker, I have never loved a Top before. Perhaps Marcus will comfort me in a few decades, when my sweet Matthew dies, when I find myself alone on Mount Storm, my West Virginia retreat, face streaked with tears, sorrow the color of Zinfandel, while snow drifts outside, sculpted by the mountain winds. Perhaps Marcus and I will preside while hillfolk neighbors bring in comfort food: potato salad, fried chicken, deviled eggs, macaroni and cheese, cherry pie, banana pudding. We'll lift glasses of black sambuca to all the brief beauties we have reluctantly and irresistibly loved. Perhaps together we will tend Matt's grave. Stubborn, cussed, and handsome as Matt is, I will probably plant purple thistles atop his ashes.

Well, that will be years yet. There it is now, the full moon, the disk of bruised bone. It rises over the eastern hills, the silhouettes of buildings. Ah, shit. I wipe tears off my unshaven cheeks. Pulling my thumb from my thrall's fervent mouth, I rise, lifting him into my arms. "Time you were crucified," I snarl. Turning my back on all of history, I carry him inside.

McDiarmid

Welton B. Marsland

There was neither lock nor bolt on the door of the third-floor apartment. This told me that the occupant was either foolhardy and careless or too poor to own anything worth locking up. I walked in and allowed my eyes to adjust to the weak light supplied by a small oil lamp standing on the crowded table in the middle of the room.

The studio was strewn end to end with the tools and creations of an artist. And this artist's talent was immediately apparent. Dark, vibrant colours and bold outlines depicted disturbing subjects on some canvases and carefully captured portraits on others. And beneath the dusty window, on a bed that looked especially uncomfortable, lay the man who had created them all.

I took the lamp from the table and brought it nearer the bed so as to take in every detail of his exquisite beauty. He was every bit as lovely as my own darling Josquin, but his face held none of the feminine qualities of that dear boy. 'Handsome,' however, was too harsh a word for him.

Moreover, he had the soft but masculine beauty that one might associate with male saints in a religious painting.

His face was a perfectly white canvas for the dark detail of his features. Thin red lips, finely arched eyebrows, and silken black hair fell lovingly onto a slightly knitted brow, suggesting a less-than-peaceful slumber. Above his high cheekbones lay long black lashes, glistening slightly with moisture that matted them lightly together. I wondered if he had cried himself to sleep that night. How long did I stand above his bed, my eyes greedily devouring him? His delicate hands were callused by arduous hours with a paintbrush. His slim body—a tantalising glimpse of hairless chest revealed by missing buttons on his shirt. Various interesting fragrances also held me entranced as my heightened olfactory sense identified them all with one breath. Neglected wine spilled on the floor. Drying paint. Brushes soaking in turpentine. The acrid aroma of sex wafted up from the bedclothes. And above all of these, the most wonderful scent of all, his blood.

I placed the lamp on the window sill, rested one knee on the bed, and leaned over to kiss his neck. Always, I believed this. Always, I told myself, moving towards an outstretched throat, "Just a kiss, then I'll leave them alone." Always, my killer instinct betrayed my good intentions. Before I could create even the semblance of a kiss on that beautiful white neck, my teeth broke the skin, my hands becoming talons on the young man's shoulders as I ripped at his flesh. He cried as he woke beneath me, his body lifting off the bed to fight me. But I held him helpless as I drank, and after a few thrashing seconds, he lay still, sobbing indecipherable words quietly into my ear.

My mind was awash with the sensual ecstasy of feeding, so it wasn't until his skin broke into the death sweat and his blood flowed more slowly into my mouth that my mind cleared a little. It was only then I discerned what he had been whispering to me all the while.

"Thank you." He spoke it so clearly but intimately that I may have said the word myself.

Becoming fully conscious once more, I realised how close he was to death and so gently disengaged myself from his neck and his desperate embrace. Laying my ear to his heart, I listened as the dull thumping ground wearily to a halt; then I stood up.

His eyes were brilliant sea green, but they stared vacantly at me now as I reached out to close them forever. As I turned from this task, my gaze fell upon three paintings at one end of the studio. Stepping over canvases and books, I moved towards them until I was close enough to hold the light to the triptych before me.

The three paintings ran in sequence. The first showed a man mourning by the side of his lover's open coffin. The second showed the man flung backwards across the coffin whilst his lover, now an awakened vampyre, fed upon him as I had just done to the artist. And the third held the most erotic but love-filled image I could imagine. The man and his vampyre lover were making passionate love on the floor, and, having cut his own breast, he let the blood drip into his beloved's gasping mouth. My head swam to think that a mortal man had, first imagined and then created these images. What a fantasy! If only he knew.

What was this long-dormant emotion daring to flutter inside me now? Jealousy? It felt a little like that, though whether it was directed at whatever love had inspired the artist to create such breath-taking works, or at the creative talent this artist clearly had possessed, I was unsure.

In one corner of each work flowed the name of their artist, the man I had just taken from life. I felt tears begin to slide down my face as I attached the name to the corpse on the bed.

McDiarmid.

In all my years of feeding and killing, I had never before known the names of any of my victims. For me, they had all been as anonymous as fatted cattle and swine are to the mortal men who feed on them. Now, I beheld the corpse of a young man whose great physical beauty and gift at art I had greatly admired. And now, I knew his name. He was no longer another of my anonymous victims; he was McDiarmid, the artist.

And I had killed McDiarmid.

Stupefied, I found myself back by his bed. I lifted the upper half of his body and eased myself underneath so that I sat with McDiarmid's head nestled in my lap. With the dead artist gathered up in my arms, I rocked mindlessly back and forth on the bed, my sobs choking on my tears. My hands caressed his firm breast, his stilled face, his fragrant hair. Splash after splash of red-tinged water fell from my face onto his. The room moved in on me, frightening me, making me move back until I was firm against the wall behind the bed.

Presently, I became aware of my troubled breathing, and slowly, slowly, it began to steady itself. My body stopped shuddering, and the torrent of tears abated until, finally, I was calm once more. With barely another sound or thought, I manoeuvred my body on top of McDiarmid's, holding myself just above him with my arms.

He was still deliciously warm, his lips still soft and inviting. So I touched them with my own. A chill coursed through me as I allowed my kiss to linger on his lips. Necrophile! I was kissing a corpse!

I lifted my face from his to study him again. Naturally, nothing about him had changed. Death had not marred his beauty in the least. If anything, he had become even more enchanting. It was that ethereal glow that I had seen on the dead before. That delicate, unearthly whiteness that emanates from them before they begin to turn blue. It was the colour and condition of my own dead skin, the only difference being that mine would never turn blue or freeze. Realising this reminded me that I myself was a walking corpse. What sin, therefore, could there possibly be in me loving McDiarmid's dead body? Necrophilia was a mortal taboo, and I was no longer mortal.

So, I loved him.

I kissed his mouth until my lips were sore. I fumbled with his clothes and mine until we were flesh on flesh, from sternums to cocks to toes. I embraced him fiercely and felt my nipples harden against him. I even held his penis in my mouth, willing it back to life with my tongue.

Of course, he remained unmoved by my caresses, and my futile seduction came abruptly to an end when I glimpsed myself in the window's reflection and was flooded with pity for my fall from grace.

I dressed hurriedly, carelessly, trying not to give another thought to the thing on the bed. I focused solely on the remarkable triptych the artist had painted, lugging the canvases outside with me before returning momentarily to the studio to overturn the oil lamp.

Let the Night Inside

L.A. Fields

One boy's tragedy was another boy's ticket to the prestigious Timber Valley Preparatory School.

Located in upstate New York, the school was just close enough to Manhattan to be plausibly nearby to most boys' wheeling-and-dealing parents but not so close that said parents ever popped over for anything less than a birthday of significance. Benjamin Copeland had been on the waitlist for this academy since elementary school and successfully tested as 'good at taking tests.' He was running out of time to get this place on his academic resume before college, but then Toby Waller went missing, and a room opened up.

He moved in on a Friday afternoon, a tiny little room with a long twin bed, a desk with a lamp, a chair, a bureau, a phone, a trash can, and a recycling bin for the future. He had access to wifi and no roommate to put up with. There were worse places to be, and he'd only be there a year before graduating early and starting college as a sophomore at the tender age of seventeen. He was a very driven young man on paper. In reality, he was just highly organized and compulsive at completing lists, tasks, and achievements. Benjamin finished everything as soon as possible, and a lot was possible with assistance from tutors and online classes.

Toby Waller was a different kind of student. Benjamin found that out when the missing boy visited him that night.

The story of what happened to Toby was annoyingly incomplete for Benjamin when he was first told of it. *The Locked Room Mystery of the Vacant Room* was how Benjamin thought of it; somebody call Sherlock Holmes. Two days into a new semester, Toby disappeared out of a room that was locked from within. His desk lamp was left on, his homework had barely begun, and his playlist was still blasting through his headphones, but Toby was gone. His wallet was still in his backpack, his clothes still on his floor, and while his window was open, his room was on the fifth floor, and all windows above the first floor could only be cracked, not flung wide (a guard against teen suicide). There was no big vent he could crawl through, no trap door or Shawshank escape hole behind a poster. No one knew where he went, and they couldn't even think of new invasive security measures to react with. The dorms were locked for 24 hours a day, and every child checked into and out of every location based on their electronic IDs, which let them into each room. A curfew already said everyone had to be in their building by 7 pm, out of the common rooms by 9 pm, and inside their own rooms by 10 pm. The security cameras in the hallway showed no one went into or came out of Toby's room after bedtime. It was a hell of a story.

The fringe websites believed this was an alien abduction. The students on campus already believed his room was haunted, and some crossed themselves as they passed by the door or a gazed at its window from the lawn. Benjamin didn't like the attention but didn't mind it too much since the new kid always got stared at a bit anyway. What he did mind was learning that they were right.

Tap, tap, tap. The sound of wind bowing the glass in the window, perhaps, Benjamin didn't notice the first round of knocks.

Tap, tap, tap, tap. Now that was concerning, but Benjamin had his back turned and didn't want to make the effort to roll over only to find some prankster using a hockey stick to tap on his window from the left or right neighboring rooms.

Tap. Tap. Tap. Deliberate, and this time a little creepy. The dark was scarier than the day, after all. Sometimes Benjamin would imagine someone was waiting to ambush him from the closet at night. Sometimes he watched too many ghost movies with staring spirits just outside of center frame, and then he couldn't fall asleep comfortably. Tonight, he wondered, *Is this ghost going to keep me up at night? Not cool, I have to be sharp for my exams.* Then, a voice coming through the two-inch crack allowed for brisk fall air.

"Hey, you up? You don't have to talk to me, but don't ignore me, bro."

Benjamin rolled over. He had moved his bed directly beneath the window, mostly because he liked the idea of sleeping more or less under the sky, waking up to see the day right above him, watching rain or leaves or snow fall from the cozy comfort of his pillows and blankets. That night, his first night in a strange new place, a boy was watching him in front of the stars. A boy who still looked like the picture in the news reports: dirty blond curls on top of his head, a turned-up nose, and a self-conscious smile.

Nope, Benjamin thought, before slamming his eyes shut. No way that was real; that's just a little anxiety dream, a little hallucination due to being displaced again for the sake of having all the advantages in life. Whenever he opened his eyes

again, there would be nothing, and Benjamin would use his not-inconsiderable self-discipline to think of other, pleasanter things before bed. The feeling of skiing, of flying down through clean, white snow, perhaps. Or his room at home, full of all his familiar things, his decorations, his childhood toys. Or even better, the hot security agent at the airport who'd given him a full-body pat-down right in front of his father. That had been quite a dirty little thrill; he could play that out in porno fashion, include a cavity search and all that jazz.

"Really?" The voice was not gone, only sullen. "Sorry I'm bothering you, okay? I'm just so lonely, and this was my room. Now you're in it. Where am I supposed to stay? I think you have to invite me in, though; there's like… some kind of force field that wasn't here before."

The whining quickly killed Benjamin's fear about things that go bump in the night. Things that go bump and then complain about how they always stub their toes weren't so terrifying.

Benjamin opened his eyes.

"There you are! What's your name?" asked Toby Waller, missing and presumed not-okay. He bobbed gently in the window's, and Benjamin slowly understood why. There was no real ledge; it was a fifth-floor window with nothing to stand on, and Toby was too far away to be on some long ladder. Ergo: Toby Waller could float.

Benjamin sat up in bed and noticed that he was woefully underdressed in nothing but boxers, but he didn't feel like he was the one making a *faux pas* in this situation. One can't come to a stranger's window and criticize them for how they dress in their own home, no no.

"Are you scared?" Toby asked. "Don't be scared, my name's Toby."

"I know," Benjamin said. "People think you're dead."

"I also think I am dead, but it suits me, wouldn't you say?" Toby did the sort of flip forward that astronauts do while floating in space, then righted himself and moved closer to the window to speak *sotto voce* with Benjamin. "I haven't talked to anyone in so long; the rest of them know me too well around here. It didn't seem smart."

"How are you doing that, the flying?" Benjamin asked.

"It's easy," Toby said, up against the glass like a prisoner trying to get as close as possible to some loved one but forbidden from touching them. "It's kind of like swimming; your body always knows how to rise to the surface if you let it."

"Tell that to everyone who's drowned," Benjamin said.

Toby laughed. There were lethal-looking fangs in his smile. "You're funny. Invite me in, won't you?"

"Let me guess, you promise you don't bite?" Benjamin asked.

"I'd ask first," Toby said. "I'm all about consent."

Benjamin smiled back. Was this boy teasing him or flirting with him? Seducing or suckering him? It was too early to tell.

"You're funny too," he said. "My name's Benjamin." He stuck his hand through the window for a shake, but the bloodlust that transformed Toby's smiling face into a furious predator's mask caused him to snatch it back before Toby could touch it.

Toby tried to reach through the window to grab it back, but whatever force allowed him to float also barred him from entry without an invitation. Benjamin was not interested in offering one after that close call. Here was a guy who seemed nice enough, but not every dog was for petting; some were wolves.

"Ben, Benjamin, bro, I'm so sorry, I didn't mean... I mean, I know what that must have looked like; I can't help how I feel." Toby was pleading, his lips right at the window's opening, placing him below Benjamin on the outside, like someone begging on their knees. "You just...you smell so good. You couldn't, maybe, like, bleed on something and let me have a taste, could you?"

"That's a bit much to ask on a first date," Benjamin murmured, but Toby heard him loud and clear.

"Ha," he said, trying to drag a smile back onto his face, looking absolutely forlorn. "You can't trust me now, can you? I get it; I get that. You're a smart guy, good for you."

"You aren't starving, are you?" Benjamin asked, quick to feel sympathy for the devil. It's possible this was a learned reflex, as the sort-of boyfriend he'd had before the summer, Eli, was always looking for pity. Eli had to stay closeted, you see, which meant they couldn't go on dates or tell anyone they were together, and if Benjamin was out to his parents and friends, that was privilege, and if Benjamin really loved Eli, he wouldn't ask for anything in exchange for giving what Eli wanted, which was blowjobs. To date, that was the extent of his sexual history, giving head and getting jerked around, literally and figuratively. It hadn't been great, but it had been slightly better than nothing.

"No, there are animals in the woods," Toby said. "But it's like...salad instead of steak. I'm fine, though, don't worry about me, I'll live."

Benjamin smiled. "Interesting way to put it."

"Right? Force of habit. I wonder if people who go blind suddenly keep accidentally saying, 'see ya later,' that kind of stuff."

Toby wiped his bangs from his brow, trying to cool himself down, collect his passions. The moonlight struck his face in full. That is when Benjamin realized that the whites of his eyes were red, bloody red.

"I see what you mean," Benjamin said.

*

They talked for a few hours that first night, which caused Benjamin to be noticeably tired during his campus tour the next day. His eyes were a little bloodshot themselves, though far from the hemorrhage-red of Toby's. He was mildly lectured about getting enough sleep and recommended chamomile tea before bed if he had insomnia. Electric kettles were allowed in the dorms, but not hot plates. Sleeping pills would not be made available to anyone under eighteen.

The topics with Toby began with "What are you in for?" i.e., why did your parents banish you here instead of raising you themselves? They also discussed who were the popular kids around and why, the bullies and why, and how much crossover there was between the two groups. Benjamin asked about the homework load, and which teachers were the petty tyrants who needed extra subservience to give out a good grade. He never got around to asking how Toby became what he was, but it was the first question he had on Saturday night.

"What happened to you?" Benjamin asked when the *tap tap tap* returned. "How'd you get out of this room? The door was locked and the window is too small."

"I can show you if you invite me in?" A beat, as Benjamin was not prepared to do that yet, or possibly at all. "Fine, be a tease. The window is not too small for a bat."

"Really? You're old-school like that? You can turn into a bat?" Benjamin was smiling. *Interview with the Vampire*, eat your heart out. "What about your clothes? Did you stuff them through the window first? Do you keep them in a tree or something when you're off doing bat business?"

"These clothes are an illusion, my go-to outfit, I feel naked without it." Toby was wearing sneakers with little bungee cords instead of laces, two layered shirts under a zip-up hoodie, and jeans with holes in the knees. He had on clothes he would only have been allowed to wear during the weekend after-school hours, as they were emphatically not part of the uniform.

"Change for me," Benjamin said. "Please."

"Bleed on something for me, please," Toby replied.

Benjamin wondered if this wasn't some old lore he was messing with, like what if one taste of his blood meant he would always be haunted by this school-boy ghoul-boy wherever he went? But maybe that could be managed anyway. It might be nice to have a familiar of the night to help him cheat at cards, madden his enemies, steal from the wicked, etc.

"Yeah, alright, hold on." Benjamin retrieved a sharp pair of scissors from the cup on his desk and a slip of toilet paper from the roll he kept as tissues on his bedside table and returned to the window. In full sight of a lustful Toby, Benjamin slid the blade a few times over the meatier part of his left forearm, just under his elbow. Girls with eating disorders sometimes did this sort of cutting, a perfect excuse if anyone spotted it, just say, *I'm a girl and I have an eating disorder.* The solution isn't punishment—just a lot of therapy that would ultimately be successful just in time for graduation.

Thin beaded lines of blood rose up, and Benjamin laid a clean square of toilet paper over them like a bandage. Up soaked the blood, and down went Toby's gaze, zeroing in.

"Will this work?" Benjamin asked. "You can digest paper?"

"I mean, I couldn't really digest paper when I dropped acid once, but the blotter went in my mouth all the same," Toby said. "Slip it to me?"

Benjamin guessed he was going first since Toby didn't seem able to focus on much else. He nudged his bloody scrap over the window sill with the back of a pencil, just in case Toby was feeling grabby.

Toby put the tissue paper on his tongue the way a still-human person might lay a thin strip of fresh sashimi in their mouth, a piece of translucently cut fish they would savor before swallowing for as long as possible. What had Benjamin's aunt told him? That 'sashimi' translated to 'pierced meat' or 'pierced body' and was not like the sushi or nigiri options on the table, because rice was not involved at all.

Sashi-me, is more like it, Benjamin thought, followed by, *What a carnivorous word.*

Toby floated as he enjoyed his delicacy and leaned back like he was adrift atop water. Benjamin waited. He had all night to burn this time, there was nothing to do on Sunday but skip the bus some students took to a local church. The school was originally founded as a Catholic institution, but in these modern times, attendance at church service wasn't mandatory. "Though most parents prefer their students participate, and we like to encourage it," his guidance counselor said. Benjamin's parents were Episcopalians in name only, and Benjamin was more interested in this blood-drinking incubus than the zombie on the cross.

When Toby came back, a lot happier once he'd tasted the good stuff, he asked, "So what'll it be, for the clothes? You want me to generate some ruffles and a wig, a nice period costume? Don't know how accurate I can get this stuff if it's my imagination that makes it and not yours. If it's mine, I can do a lot of battle gear from video games but not much else. Or, I could do no clothes. Do you want to see me naked?"

Benjamin knew his answer was 'yes, very much so,' but he still felt the need to be coy. "I mean...would you mind, particularly? Would you like that?"

"I don't mind," Toby murmured. "No skin off my back, you know. Do you want me to like it?" Toby zipped off his imaginary hoodie and dropped it to the side, where it promptly disappeared with no puff, no outline, just gone in a blink.

"I want an honest answer," Benjamin said.

"Alright," Toby said, returning closer to the window. "The last time I was naked outside, it was because I got tricked into skinny-dipping at summer camp, and the other guys stole my clothes."

"Was that traumatizing?" Benjamin asked.

"At first, but I had time to think on the walk back to the cabins, and by the time I got there, I thought it's only embarrassing if I'm embarrassed, right? So I just strolled up to my bunk, naked as a jaybird, cock of the walk."

"Then what happened?"

"I got in trouble for agreeing to skinny-dip, but they got in more trouble for doing the same plus bullying. We all got expelled from camp, but they got labeled as sexual victimizers, and good luck getting into the Ivy Leagues with that on the record. Rumors can be ignored with enough money, but they have to live with a paper trail."

Benjamin wondered what that victory truly meant, since Toby wouldn't make it into any college now, but instead, he asked, "You went to school here all year and had to go to summer camp?"

"Busy parents," Toby said, before backing up again. He pulled his shirts off next, which made his hair bounce. "Anyway, I'm really not shy anymore, but if you want more in this vein, I'll want more of what's in your veins, if that's okay with you."

Toby had a smile that suggested he knew very well that this was a bargain Benjamin would find enticing. Preternatural hunch, or could he read Benjamin's thoughts? Maybe he could tell when a person's heart quickened or when their pupils dilated and their blood vessels gorged, and he made an educated guess.

"I'd... I'm not saying no," Benjamin said, "but I'd have some more questions first."

"Questions like what?" Toby kicked his shoes off, plucked socks one and two from his feet and tossed them into nonexistence like petals off a daisy. Next, he unbuttoned his jeans.

Benjamin sighed and put his hand over his crotch. The window sill was at nipple-height as Benjamin kneeled on his bed, but surely Toby still knew what he was doing down there. Benjamin was stroking, squeezing, and wondering what it would be like to get into Toby's pants himself. He couldn't think clearly enough to ask that out loud, however, and really his first questions should be more along the lines of, 'Are you going to kill me if I let you in?' When Benjamin ultimately remained silent, Toby continued.

"You write out all your questions then, okay?" Toby said, dropping his pants into gravity's darkness. All that remained was his underwear, white and lumpy with his equipment just under the fabric. Another pressing question arose: If those clothes were a hallucination, was the body flesh? Was it hot or cold? Could it still... do stuff?

When Toby popped his member out into the calm night air, it looked solid enough to make an impact, hard enough to leave a mark.

Sunday night, and it wasn't too sacred a day to keep the vampires at bay. In fact, it was time for the big Q&A.

Q: Is vampirism infectious? What about other forms of blood-borne diseases?

A: A vampire can't carry disease because disease feeds on life, and vampires are dead. You can't become a vampire without being on the absolute edge of death and consuming enough regurgitated vampire blood for the change-over to take hold. Your body doesn't want to die, but it doesn't want living death either, so it will only take it as a last resort.

Q: Can you control yourself enough to feed without killing?

A: Yes.

Q: How can you be sure?

A: There aren't a lot of dead cows at the dairy farms nearby, that's how I'm sure.

Q: How did you become a vampire?

A: Last summer, a woman found me, said she was my mother. I was adopted. I thought I was dreaming her. I invited her in night after night, whenever she came, until one night I think she took too much. I felt cold, I passed out, I think she realized because she started saying, "Oh shit, oh shit," and the next day I was driven up here in the dark, dropped off in my room, and realized pretty quickly that I had a severe allergy to sunlight. I hid all day, I escaped at night.

Q: As a bat. How did you know how to do that?

A: I didn't, I haven't been able to do it since. I think the panic took over because I wanted to escape so bad but didn't know how without going through the hallway, the other boys... I wanted to murder them. I got out and killed a couple of rabbits instead, the next night a raccoon. They found me missing, they searched the woods, which is when I moved to the farm. When they gave up on me, I kept trying to get back in my room, wanted to sleep on a mattress. Then you arrived, and now it's your room.

Q: Do you think that vampire lady was actually your mom?

A: I don't know. Maybe she wasn't, maybe she was just a liar who killed me on accident and revived me out of guilt or double accident. Maybe she was my mother, and she was a bad one, which is why she gave me up in the first place and then screwed up her second chance too.

Q: Do you actually like me? Do you now or have you ever liked boys? Or are you hungry, and I just happen to be in your old room?

A: I like you. I was probably gearing up to be bi- or pan- or omni-sexual. I don't know, it doesn't matter anymore.

Q: Because we're all delicious to you now?

A: Yes, but you're my only friend.

Q: I want to be more than friends with you. You know that, right? I want to have sex with you.

A: Actually, you want me to have sex with you, and that's exactly what I want too. I want to penetrate you in every sense of the word.

Q: Does it hurt? Getting fed on?

A: After the initial pinch, it's like a dream. A really good, loving, funny, erotic, refreshing dream. They don't make drugs that good yet.

Q: Can we go slow?

A: Of course. I've got all the time in the world.

Benjamin was not prepared to invite the night inside his sanctuary on the first try, but he did decide it was time for that handshake they skipped.

"If I give you my wrist to bite, you won't take the hand off?" he asked. "I won't be the second mysterious fate in this room when they find me bled out, wrist torn open, a messy suicide?"

"I'll feed on a forest creature first, so I'm not ravenous. Does that help?" Toby asked.

"If I can watch you do it, I guess so."

While Toby was away finding his sacrificial victim, Benjamin wrote down a 'this was not a suicide' note just in case the night went poorly. When Toby returned holding a fox in his arms like a baby, an animal as docile as a domesticated puppy, Benjamin suddenly had more questions.

"You've mesmerized him," Benjamin said.

"Her," Toby corrected.

"How?"

"I bit her first; she likes it like you'll like it." Toby flew closer and laid the creature on the sill between them.

She was cat-like and wolf-like all at once, beautiful. Benjamin had never seen one up close before.

"Vixen," he said. "Female foxes, I think they're called vixens."

"That's hot," Toby said with a smirk.

"I don't want you to kill her," Benjamin said. "How about showing me you can feed a little and then stop, okay?"

"Okay."

"And you're sure you can't bite me and then hypnotize me to invite you in, right?"

"I mean, if I could hypnotize you, I would have done it the first night," Toby said with a shrug. "Maybe a more mature vampire could, but I can't."

Toby was giving the fox affectionate little scritches as he spoke. Benjamin dared to touch her tail, which had unfurled into his room and waved lazily and contentedly. She certainly wasn't scared or in pain, even though she was wounded, captured, and five stories up, and should have been wild with panic.

"Alright, go ahead then," Benjamin said.

He watched. From his front-row seat, he was close enough to smell the forest on the fox's coat, as well as the tang of blood in Toby's mouth as he sunk his teeth into the vixen's neck. She went limp, her tummy unprotected under the moonlight, and possibly had a smile on her face, but foxes always had that long grin, didn't they? That didn't mean anything. Toby's teeth seemed to elongate out of his gums like snake's fangs or cat's claws, and they retracted back in when he was done. His bloody eyes were watching Benjamin watch him the whole time.

Benjamin knew relying on Toby's answers was suspect. Based on looks, he could probably be sure this was the same boy who was alive last month, so it was true he was a new vampire in that sense, but... then again, 'Toby' had already proven his skill in illusion work, so what was actually, objectively true? Couldn't a demon have kicked out Toby's soul and taken his body? Couldn't Toby be so desperate for human blood that he'd say anything to get a little? It's not like there was a safe-sex method to a bloodsport like this. What if Toby could infect him? What if the fox's blood carried some new pandemic, and Benjamin decided to become patient zero, another Typhoid Mary? But then again, you had to take some chances in life, didn't you? And this was the most interesting offer Benjamin had ever had.

Toby stopped feeding. He licked his lips, kissed the vixen's forehead, and raised his head even with Benjamin's again.

"She's still alive, check."

Benjamin did so. He felt her heartbeat in her chest, felt her breath on his cheek, and both were even and deep, not ragged or shallow. Benjamin also kissed the vixen on her forehead. The brush of her ear beneath his chin was as soft as crushed velvet.

He was ready.

"Okay, take her home, and then we'll try something," Benjamin said.

While Toby was gone, Benjamin brushed his teeth. He wondered whether he should bother since surely a vampire's breath would smell like rotting blood, but he figured it was better to be safe than paranoid about it. He wetted his face and hair with the same spray bottle he kept for brushing his teeth alone, rather than visit the communal bathroom for trivial grooming. He folded his 'not a suicide' note and slid it in his door frame, just above the latch and bolt, so it would fall at the feet of anyone who opened the door but would otherwise remain unseen. He kneeled on his bed and waited, watching the window like he was expecting the Annunciation of the second coming of Christ. Water to wine, wine to blood, bread to body, dust to flesh to dust again... unless you make a deal with the devil.

Speaking of, Toby returned with what looked like love in his eyes. He waited for Benjamin to speak first. Benjamin opened his mouth and hesitated, knowing this could be his last chance to back out. Toby nodded encouragement, and Benjamin rose up on his knees.

"I think we can shake hands now," Benjamin said. "And you can drink a little from my wrist. Is that okay?"

"Perfect," Toby said, before literally licking his chops.

Benjamin took a deep breath and stuck his hand outside. It was the last coherent decision he ever made.

Toby moved fast, grabbed the hand proffered to him, and sunk his teeth into the underbelly of Benjamin's wrist. The moment the tips were in, Benjamin started to swoon. It was like the one time he gave blood without eating breakfast first and started to pass out, except that exsanguination didn't give him a boner, and this one did.

Benjamin moaned and slumped on the window sill, which extended his whole arm into the dark of the night. Toby took that as further permission, sinking his teeth into Benjamin's elbow crook. Benjamin would have expected a loss of blood to feel cold, as it had in the blood-mobile outside of his old high school, but this felt warm, liquid, molten. His moan turned into panting whimpers.

Toby raised his head, mouth rouged, eyes bright red instead of dark red, full of new blood. He kissed his way up Benjamin's arm towards his shoulder, leaving rose petals of bloody lip imprints as he went. When he was as close as he could be to Benjamin's ear, he whispered to him. "Invite me in," he said. "Please, I know you want to, I know you want me with you, on top of you, inside of you, I can hear it clanging like a bell, your heart..." Toby rolled his eyes back as if the sound was shaking his blood, brain, and bones.

"You can't fit," Benjamin said, thinking simultaneously that Toby couldn't squeeze through the window, and also of his thick cock, it couldn't possibly fit, not easily, not painlessly, no way.

"At least let me try." A kiss at Benjamin's elbow, his wrist, then the back of his hand, as sweetly as Toby had kissed the vixen's sleek head, a gentlemanly move. "If I can't get in, oh well, but if I can, me and you, all night...."

Benjamin wanted that, all night with this guy all to himself, inside and out, no one squeamish about 'I can't put my fingers in there, it's too dirty' or 'it's gross to want that in your mouth.' For years Benjamin had wanted a boyfriend, and the first one he got acted like sex was a hassle, messier in real life than the pornos led him to believe, icky. And now Toby had already tasted Benjamin and wanted more. Benjamin wanted that too.

He felt drunk. Though Benjamin had not yet been fully drunk on alcohol, he understood that this was what it would be like: a pleasant dizziness, his inhibitions only a speck in the rearview mirror, and a reckless feeling of immortality, which, considering what he was dealing with, could be where he was headed. Who didn't want to stay forever young? Who didn't want to be truly ravaged at least once before they died?

"Alright," Benjamin said, bringing back his arm, steadying himself, and forcing the window as open as it could be: two inches tall and two feet wide. He leaned back, felt the world tilt with him, and then said, "Come in."

Toby flew back, setting himself up for a sort of running start. Benjamin watched as long as he could while Toby flew towards him again, sure that he was about to crash and crunch into the window, shaking the wall. But as he got closer, Toby seemed to narrow, concentrating to a point. Benjamin threw himself back against his pillow, afraid of being smashed into. It was a wise decision on his part because a bat zoomed in like a flung dart and smacked against the far side of his wall.

"Oh, no," Benjamin said, his mind skipping to concern for the poor bitty bat that just crash-landed. Then, that bat started to seize and grow.

Chest up like the bat was being shocked with heart-starter paddles, then bigger. It sat up, and then it was the size of a backpack, looking like a strange and disturbing plush toy. Another heave to stand, toddler-height, before it wrapped itself in one large wing and spun. After one full revolution, it stood tall. When the wing came down like a cloak, it revealed Toby, naked as if fresh from a cocoon. Toby's crimson eyes goggled around once, then focused on Benjamin.

Benjamin felt a pulse of fear rip through him, almost enough to sober him up from whatever voodoo was in Toby's bite. Here was this Prince of Hell, suddenly looming over him in a locked room, in a remote place far from anything familiar to Benjamin. What had he done? Was it something that could never be undone?

When Toby fell on him, Benjamin thought he was already dead. Those fangs in his jugular, his consciousness fading away as his tendons were severed, his bones disarticulated, and his own blood pooled around him. Those would be his final moments, he was sure of it, but then it didn't happen that way.

Toby fell on him and kissed him, his tongue a hot arrowhead in Benjamin's mouth, filling it with the taste of blood, like pennies and marinara sauce. When Benjamin realized he was being kissed and not consumed, he put his arms around Toby's back, his legs around Toby's body. Their eyes met, and then they both looked down at the flesh pressed between them, their members side-by-side, and at least for Benjamin, as insanely sensitive as if it had been degloved of skin, nothing but screamingly raw nerves, flayed alive.

"You won't kill me," Benjamin said, daring to believe it. He kissed his midnight friend on the mouth, the cheek, the neck.

"You don't ever have to die, not with me," Toby said. His eyes feasted over Benjamin's body before his mouth dipped down to do a little of the same. He covered each nipple with his lips before sinking his teeth in for a taste here, a taste there. Then, he used his tongue to draw a sticky line of red towards Benjamin's bellybutton. It looked like warpaint.

"Don't bite that," Benjamin said as Toby's eyes rested on his cock.

Toby only smiled and picked up Benjamin's knees. He set the head of his cock against Benjamin's entrance and nudged at it tentatively.

"Invite me in," Toby said.

Benjamin's nethers felt like a boiling pot that had to be turned down or allowed to boil over. He'd put things up there before: the handle of a hairbrush, of a hammer, and once a slick, rounded lady's conditioner bottle, glassy with curves. Each of those items had felt interesting enough, but they were never quite right: too many angles, too cold, and in the end, too inert every time. Now on top of him was Toby, hot with his own fire or filled with Benjamin's warmth, powerful, enthusiastic, and as starved for this as Benjamin was. Their desire was equal.

Benjamin was too far gone to articulate all of that. He only nodded before saying once more, "Come in."

It didn't hurt like he thought it would. Instead of pain at the rim, his ring, Toby's cock somehow managed to slither through like some cephalopod, it could compress a lot of soft tissue and tentacles through the mouth of a glass bottle. Instead, the overwhelming sensation was heat, as if Benjamin's insides were injected with lava.

Toby entered to the hilt, then paused and watched Benjamin acclimate to this new intrusion. "You never have to die," Toby said. "You can come with me, come to the woods, stay with me and my mother. She didn't abandon me, she never did, really. That was just a story. She was transformed when I was a baby; she waited until I was old enough to join her. You could join us too, you know. Your parents abandoned you here. That never has to happen again."

Benjamin heard Toby speak, then looked down at himself, naked and painted and wide-open and unashamed. Could he stay this natural, proud, and fulfilled forever? Could he really say no, that he'd rather button up again, go to class, and get a job, all to impress the parents who've been waiting a lifetime for their son to be somebody of substance? Was this body not enough, just as it was at that moment?

He looked back to Toby and said, "Kiss me."

Toby's hips began to thrust, a piston engine revving up. His body fell like a cloak again, this time over Benjamin's. They kissed and nipped at one another, and as his pleasure started to crest, Benjamin clawed at Toby's back, cutting scratches like wings across his shoulders, wings for a boy who could fly. Toby's next kiss covered Benjamin's entire mouth. As Benjamin came, hands-free and ecstatic, Toby's curved teeth penetrated his top lip first, then his bottom, stapling them shut so that Benjamin's groans of pleasure could not escape.

When Benjamin didn't arrive at class the next morning, his room was unlocked and entered. The note that fell from the door perplexed investigators; the mystery of the disappearing room forced the school to pay out an undisclosed sum to Benjamin's parents and brick that unit shut, and the farms nearby had a dearth of predatory animals that they hardly noticed, except that they were pleasantly surprised.

Afterword

Steve Berman

I met my first monster during my freshman year of college when Michael beguiled me in the bathroom, and I let him hold sway over me for another three years.

On a Sunday morning, I had cut the soft pad of two fingers while whitling the handle of an old paint brush, a project for an art class. Blood started to fall drip onto the dorm room bed as well as the carpet. Back then, my heart would quicken, and I often fainted at the sight of blood—especially my own. I stumbled out and down the hall and into the communal bathroom.

A bare-chested Michael in briefs stood by the sink brushing his teeth. When he saw my bleeding fingers, he spat toothpaste into the basin, then pulled me close, trapping me between the counter and his body. The splash from the cold-water tap dampened my pajama bottoms. I looked down at the stammel drops on the laminate and the porcelain that escaped the water. I felt as if I might topple, even as Michael took my injured hand and held it under the tap. As he uttered my name, his other hand gripped me beneath my jaw; he forced me to look into the wide mirror.

I felt his cheek, unshaven, scratched my own, and breathed in the peppermint scent of his toothpaste. The rushing water chilled my fingertips and waist, so cold, my head and my back warmed by his breath, his chest, as he told me to keep my eyes on him.

I felt him stir behind me. His muscular arms moved me, making me his puppet. My underwear was soaked—I don't think with just water.

"There," he said, in the voice a father uses with a scared child. "Much better."

He allowed me to look down at my hand. Like bleached bone, the finger was so pale from being held under the cold tap. But as I watched, bright beads of blood formed at the very tip of my ring finger..

Michael tsks-tsked. He lifted my hand, and I watched in the mirror as he slid that finger into his mouth and suckled. His eyes gazed at my reflection. I moaned. He murmured. The fabric at my ass became clingy, binding us together thanks to a sudden warmth.

His teeth bit down, only a little, as if my fingertip might be a grape he was testing for sweetness. Only then did he let go of my wrist; my finger slipped from between his lips.

With his body still pressed against mine, Michael spoke into my ear. "Remember: You will never make my bed unless I tell you to." He then smacked the back of his toothbrush against my forehead. I wondered for a moment if his short hair, clipped close along one side, might feel like bristles.

Back in my dorm room, while Depeche Mode played on the stereo, Michael was cruel to me and left traces of his thirst on my shoulder, my neck, and the sheets. I was not allowed to faint until he was done with me.

And even then, he was never done with me. Not when I offered myself as a gay Friday, though I never realized how much he would demand of me. And how readily I accepted crumbs of affection and scavenged for mementos like a lovesick magpie.

During those days in New Orleans, I met many of Michael's... should I even use the word "victim"? Even if almost all seemed willing? Or was their consent an illusion granted by his charm, his swagger, his hypnotic gaze? He drank deeply from fraternity pledges, classmates, and even a graduate teaching assistant. I remember the bushy-haired kid, a thin busker devoted to his acoustic guitar. The sun browned his skin, leaving it redolent with sweat. The apartment smelled of body odor and thrift for days as Michael supped, strumming the young man's limbs. I had to clean up the mess, ignoring how my roommate joked about leftovers as I plucked an errant steel guitar string from stained bedding in the laundry bin.

I only escaped him because, with graduation, I moved away. Though I suspect now he had grown bored of me. Even Dracula dispensed with Reinfield once he became tiresome.

The half of the duplex I rented while in graduate school seemed askew as if exhausted, the walls cracked in the corners, frown lines dislodging paint. The furnishings were worn enough to suggest comfort when they needed to be replaced, and the appliances could not be trusted. That night, the kitchen faucet decided to leak and shudder as if it wanted to dance and flood the room.

I knocked on my neighbor's door. She was also my landlord. Mostly an absent landlord, as she was rarely home thanks to her dream of rising in the pyramidal ranks of Pampered Chef; when something went amiss, she would grow flustered and press a chocolate drizzler or tiny whisk into my hand as if it were the solution to a clogged drain or bad fuse, then call out to her lanky teenage son, Sawyer, to help me.

Tonight, she bribed me with a bamboo spoon, pale and almost gritty to the touch.

After grabbing his tool box, Sawyer followed me back to my kitchen.

The phone rang as I watched him scuttle backward into the open cabinet beneath the sink. I didn't recognize the pained man's voice on the line who told me Michael was dead. Only after the second aborted sob did I realize Michael's father, a reserved man who I had only met twice, must have asked my parents for my number.

As the elastic of the cord swaying between me and the wall creaked from age, as if it might snap before I heard how Michael died, I looked down at Sawyer. The hem of his t-shirt had risen higher to reveal the gentle curve of his stomach and the wale of soft, brown hair from belly button to crotch hidden beneath denim.

Working construction, Michael had fallen out of a second-floor window and landed on an exposed rebar. I resisted asking whether his son made a pretty corpse because I knew the answer, and the poor man grieved for a son he believed was human.

After I put the receiver down, I went into the bedroom. The unmade bed was a testament to sleepless nights—I suspected all of Michael's victims would find sleep elusive; we would stare into the darkness and feel so alone, even while we touched ourselves, along the raised scars, then down to our dicks, as a weird flush that crept up our body.

He left us addicts, craving his mouth. Now, none of us would ever be sated.

I flipped the latches on the trunk I brought to Iowa almost nine months ago. My fingers sought through the layer of sweaters and corduroys for the prairie winter and curling issues of *Blueboy, Freshman,* even the procured *Antinous* delivered from Amsterdam, a small package wrapped in butcher paper and course twine.

I unwrapped it.

"I think I fixed it." Sawyer stood in the doorway, still holding a wrench. He looked damp and disheveled from the water as if caught in a small downpour. His gaze fell to what I held in my hands. "What's that?"

I walked closer to him. "Oh, it's a little outsider art I made ages ago. A bit of soap molded around a toothbrush, wrapped in a guitar string, a beer label—"

"It's ugly." And yet, he was fascinated by the doll.

"Yes, isn't it wonderfully ugly?" I tilted my hands so that the doll rolled into his grasp when he reached for it with grimy fingers.

Then he winced and let loose a pained breath. The doll dropped to the floor, and we both looked at the small gash in his palm.

"Oh, sorry—there's a base screw from an old car ornament. I forget that the sharp end poked through the back." I took his hand in mine. "It's not so bad."

I put an arm around his shoulders and guided him into the bathroom.

In the mirror, a bare-chested Michael grinned as he watched both of us. The cold-water tap began to gush on its own.

"Who's that?" Sawyer said to the reflection. His voice was a whisper, a gasp. In my arms, he started to tremble, like boys do right before indulging in something awful.

My teeth hurt like I had been crunching on a sugar cube. I licked the top row and marveled at how sharp they felt on my dry tongue. Thirst wrapped my throat. "That's only me," I told Sawyer before letting my face brush against the hot skin of his neck. My lips parted. "Only me."

Donors

Steve Berman has been writing queer horror fiction for almost three decades. He did live with Michael Carte for several years—and tasted Michael on one occasion. Berman edited the Lambda Literary Award-winning anthology *His Seed*. The vampire film that had the greatest impact on an adolescent Berman would be 1958's *The Return of Dracula*. He remembers the scene where Count Dracula tries to hypnotize a young man who is protecting his girlfriend—and suddenly, the world of horror movies became homoerotic.

Benji Bright is a black, gay writer of smut with a speculative bent. He serves up explicit stories and games at http://patreon. com/benjibright and can be found on Twitter (occasionally) at @benji_bright. For more of his work, you can also check out his website, benmakesstuff.com. Benji is waiting patiently for Alucard (*Castlevania*) to float through his window and [REDACTED] the [REDACTED] out of him.

L.A. Fields is the author of two Lambda Literary Award finalists, five YA books, one short story collection, and two works of scholarship. She has an MFA and a calico cat. Her favorite vampire is the "Brat Prince," Lestat, who she finds unruly and playful, yet honestly in love with his mopey progeny.

John T. Fuller lives in the north of England with his partner and always chooses his beer by which has the best pun name. As well as writing, he enjoys rock music and trashy '80s horror films. He's currently working on a historical gay romance novel, and you can pick up a copy of his novella *When the Music Stops* or his short story collection *The Trojan Project* (jointly authored with Richard Rider) online. He is quite taken with the vampires from *The Lost Boys.*

Maxwell I. Gold is a Rhysling Award-nominated author who writes prose poetry and short stories in weird and cosmic fiction. He is a regular contributor to *Spectral Realms,* edited by Lovecraft scholar S.T. Joshi, and his work has also appeared in *Weirdbook Magazine, Space and Time Magazine, Startling Stories, Baffling Magazine,* and many others. Obviously, his ideal vampire is Polidori's Lord Ruthven.

Greg Herren is an acclaimed mystery and horror writer. His anthology, *Love, Bourbon Street,* and novel, *Murder in the Rue Dauphine,* won Lambda Literary Awards. A co-founder of the Saints and Sinners Literary Festival, he resides in New Orleans.

Eric LaRocca is the author of several works of dark fiction including *Things Have Gotten Worse Since We Last Spoke* and *The Strange Thing We Become & Other Dark Tales.* Eric's favorite vampire is one of history's most notorious and bloodthirsty icons: Countess Elizabeth Bathory. When not reading or writing tales of the macabre, Eric can be found roaming the streets of Boston, MA in search of inspiration.

Southern gentleman **Jeff Mann**'s vampire fetish began with watching Barnabas Collins on *Dark Shadows.* Jeff's stories of blood and bondage can be found in *Desire and Devour* and *Insatiable.* He has won the Lambda Literary Award twice, once for *A History of Barbed Wire* and once for *Salvation,* the second half of his Civil War romance series. He is an acclaimed poet and essayist. His most recent books are *Endangered Species* and *Redneck Bouquet*, a finalist for the Weatherford Award for Poetry.

Welton B. Marsland is a queer-punk writer from Melbourne, Australia whose stories, features, poetry, and more have appeared in many local & international markets. Debut novel *By the Currawong's Call*, set in 1890s Australia, and winner of a Bisexual Book Award. Their favorite vampire is Robert Warram from *The Undead Die* by E. Everett Evans. Keep track of Marsland on Twitter @wbmarsland.

When not writing erotica, **Kenzie Mathews** drinks too much coffee and spoils her dogs. She's had the good fortune to have stories published within two volumes of *Best Gay Erotica, Lust in Time, Best Lesbian Erotica, Best Gay Erotica Volume 4, Stranded: Boys Behaving Badly, Sexy Librarian's Dirty Thirty*, and others. Her favorite vampire is Sheridan LeFanu's Carmilla.

Whitt Pond was born in Lubbock, Texas around the time of a famous UFO sighting, which explains a lot. He has at various times been a Boy Scout, a West Point cadet, a Peace Corps volunteer, an art museum attendant, and a language tutor, but most of his adult life was spent writing software for ungrateful computers. Whitt likes to write horror stories because they are easier than screaming all the time. He likes to write erotic horror because sex scares some people more than death.

Jason Rubis lives with his family in the Washington, DC-area. His short fiction has appeared in *Weirdbook* and anthologies from Circlet Press and Mischief. He is the author of *Terror*

Birds, The World Beneath, Project Caliban, and *Jurassic Beach,* all available from Severed Press. He has a preference for Christopher Lee's portrayal of Dracula.

Cecilia Tan is an inductee to the Saints & Sinners LGBTQ Writers Hall of Fame, and her works have racked up several other awards over the years as well. She is the founder of Circlet Press, Inc., publishers of erotic science fiction and fantasy, as well as the author of many books, including the ground-breaking erotic sf/fantasy short story collections *Black Feathers* and *White Flames,* and the *Magic University* series. Her short stories have appeared in *Ms. Magazine, Asimov's Science Fiction, Absolute Magnitude, Strange Horizons,* and tons of other places. Her upcoming paranormal/urban fantasy series from The Vanished Chronicles will be published Real Soon Now. Her favorite fictional vampire has to be David Bowie's character in *The Hunger,* cellist John Blaylock.

And the editor... There is a rumor that editor **Michael Carte,** a handsome but oh-so-aggressive young man, died in a tragic accident in New Orleans in 1990. However, the publisher swears he has seen a thirsty Michael haunting several places, especially on warm, rainy nights.